MW00857045

the **americas**

also in **the americas** series

Breathing, In Dust by Tim Z. Hernandez
The Centaur in the Garden by Moacyr Scliar
Changó, the Biggest Badass by Manuel Zapata Olivella
Daughter of Silence by Manuela Fingueret
The Fish Child by Lucía Puenzo
Hut of Fallen Persimmons by Adriana Lisboa
Kafka's Leopards by Moacyr Scliar
The Last Reader by David Toscana
The Origin of Species and Other Poems by Ernesto Cardenal
Symphony in White by Adriana Lisboa
The War in Bom Fim by Moacyr Scliar
Timote by José Pablo Feinmann
Unlucky Lucky Tales by Daniel Grandbois

The Neighborhood

Gonçalo M. Tavares

Translated by Roopanjali Roy

Illustrations by Rachel Caiano

Introduction by Philip Graham

Texas Tech University Press

This book is typeset in Fairfield. The paper used in this book meets the minimum requirements of ANSI/NISO Z39.48-1992 (R1997). ♾

Designed by Kasey McBeath | Cover illustration by Rachel Caiano

Library of Congress Cataloging-in-Publication Data
Tavares, Gonçalo M., 1970–
[Bairro. English]
The neighborhood / Gonçalo M. Tavares ; translated by Roopanjali Roy ; illustrations by Rachel Caiano ; introduction by Philip Graham.
p. cm. — (The Americas)
Summary: "In six parts, the stories of Misters Valéry, Calvino, Juarroz, Henri, Kraus, and Walser are imagined through prose and illustration"—Provided by publisher.
ISBN 978-0-89672-711-3 (hardcover : alk. paper) —
ISBN 978-0-89672-805-9 (e-book)
I. Roy, Roopanjali. II. Caiano, Rachel. III. Title.
PQ9282.A89B3713 2012
869.3'5—dc23 2012023331

Funded by Direção Geral do Livro, dos Arquivos e das Bibliotecas

Printed in the United States of America
12 13 14 15 16 17 18 19 20 / 9 8 7 6 5 4 3 2 1

Texas Tech University Press
Box 41037 | Lubbock, Texas 79409-1037 USA
800.832.4042 | ttup@ttu.edu | www.ttupress.org

Contents

INTRODUCTION

This English-language version of *The Neighborhood* is a welcome introduction to the United States of an essential body of work by Gonçalo M. Tavares. One of Portugal's greatest living authors, Tavares, though just turned forty, has already carved out a place for himself in that country's literary history. Still relatively unknown in North America (Dalkey Archive published his novel *Jerusalem* in 2009), Tavares's works have won enough awards to fill a town crier's long list and have been translated and praised in over forty-five countries, including England, Spain, Italy, India, Poland, France, South Korea, Greece, Germany, and Argentina. In Portugal his works are regularly adapted as plays, oratorios, and operas.

I first became aware of Tavares's work when I attended the Ninth International Short Story Conference, which was held in Lisbon in June 2006. There was quite a buzz about him; he had won the José Saramago Prize the previous year, for his third novel, *Jerusalem*, and the Nobel Prize–wining Saramago himself wasn't shy about doling out praise: "*Jerusalem* is a great book, and truly deserves a place among the great works of Western literature. Gonçalo M. Tavares has no right to be writing so well at the age of 35. One feels like punching him!"

When I attended Gonçalo Tavares's reading at the Lisbon conference, I heard for the first time selections from his series of books (known as *Os Senhores* in Portuguese and *The Misters* in English) that make up *The Neighborhood* and was at once entranced by the economy and power of his writing. Before I'd left for Portugal, the editors of the literary journal *Hunger Mountain* had asked me to pull together a special section on contemporary Portuguese fiction from the writers I encountered at the conference, and I made the easy decision to include five brief stories from Tavares's *Mister Henri* and six from *Mister Brecht*. As fiction editor of the literary/arts journal *Ninth Letter*, I also chose for publication five selections from *Mister Valéry*. Those limited excerpts marked Tavares's first appearance in English in the United States. Now, with Texas Tech University Press's hefty volume in hand, readers in America will have the opportunity to stretch out in appreciation of Tavares's unique imaginative universe through the elegant midwifery of Roopanjali Roy's crisp translations.

It is perhaps best to introduce the uninitiated to Tavares's oeuvre by discussing the line drawings of his wife and longtime collaborator, the artist Rachel Caiano, in particular her map of *The Neighborhood,* which resembles the narrow streets and closely set buildings of a traditional Lisbon *bairro*. Caiano's map for the early editions of the series listed only four inhabitants, Misters Valéry, Henri, Brecht, and Juarroz, with so many of the surrounding apartments empty. As Tavares's project has expanded, Misters Calvino, Kraus, and then Walser were added. By now Caiano's map is happily cluttered with thirty-nine names, and though only ten Misters have yet appeared as books (and a few of them remain to be translated), they signal the series' steady future growth.

As for Caiano's illustrations within, her shifting styles echo each book's particular combination of whimsy and seriousness. Indeed many of the illustrations seem inextricably linked with the individual stories: the delicate sadness of Mister Juarroz's dresser drawer filled with emptiness, for example; or the spare lines of Mister Valéry's bowler hat; the disquieting, blocky shadows of the Boss's office in *Mister Kraus*; or the frenzied scribble that charts the friendly dismantling of Mister Walser's country house.

By now the reader of this introduction has surely noticed that all the Misters evoke the identities of important literary figures. To a certain extent their personalities work within the perimeters of what we think we know of those writers and, more important, of their writing. Mr. Calvino is of course the literary avatar of the Italian fabulist Italo Calvino; Mister Valéry is a nod to the French poet and critic Paul Valéry; Mister Juarroz is some version of the Argentinean poet Roberto Juarroz; the isolated Mister Walser (his house, one might notice, stands apart from the apartment blocks of Caiano's map) resembles Robert Walser, the troubled Swiss writer prone to long, lonely walks; Mister Kraus's stories reflect the political and linguistic outrage of the Austrian essayist Karl Kraus; and Mister Henri's tipsy self is a sliver of the neosurrealist and drug experimenter Henri Michaux. The books of *The Neighborhood* are not limited to a direct correspondence, however, but instead work out the various possibilities—personal, philosophical—of that core knowledge about the writers who have inspired Tavares. Readers familiar with the work of the Argentine poet

Roberto Juarroz will certainly enjoy Tavares's sly reference to that poet's "vertical poetry" when Mister Juarroz (who has a fear of climbing stepladders) observes, "If we keep in mind that falling is a simple shift in location, a change of the body's position along a vertical trajectory, then falls will no longer be so scary." But this inside knowledge isn't necessary to enjoy the chapter "Falling." Similarly one doesn't need to know that Karl Kraus believed that the misuse of language was equivalent to the misuse of power in order to enjoy the Boss's twisting of words in *Mister Kraus*, where the canny leader has this exchange with one of his assistants:

> "It is not enough to obtain the opinion of the people. It is necessary to interpret it. Even when they only write a cross, what does that cross mean? Each personal opinion should be interpreted under a magnifying glass, by specialists."
>
> "Who are. . . ?"
>
> "Who are what I call: Specialists in Me."

It should then come as no surprise that the Boss soon declares that the best specialist in "Me" is "Me! Me! I am the one who will objectively interpret the subjective opinion of the people."

While a certain sly humor, sometimes threaded with bitterness, as in the example above, creates an important atmosphere in the books of *The Neighborhood*, it is always paired with a philosophical sophistication and deep seriousness of intent. The individual pieces can be read quickly, but they also reward slower consideration and rereading. In many cases, the books teach the reader how to read them. The humor urges us on, but slowly we come to understand that the humor resembles a koan-like take on the world, one where personal, logical, and political absurdities are displayed in such a way that they seem to deconstruct themselves and yet, miraculously, stay constructed. Mister Juarroz, who values thinking over the sensory incursions of the world, has a favorite drawer that he fills with emptiness, much to the frustration of his long-suffering wife. Mister Valéry is very short, but because he jumps a lot, he can say, "I am just like any tall person, except for less time."

The genius of Tavares's work is that its profundities are clothed in a deceptively simple style and therefore can be appreciated by a wide range of readers. To this point I offer anecdotal evidence. My daughter Hannah, eleven years old when my family and I lived for a year in Lisbon, loved his books. Gonçalo was kind enough to agree to give a reading at her Portuguese school, and when he arrived the sixth-graders offered him a surprise performance, enacting with great brio several of the stories from *The Neighborhood* books. I was mightily impressed by how even young children could be moved by Tavares's writing, even though they certainly hadn't a clue who Juarroz, Valéry, or the others might be.

As most critics agree, Tavares's imaginative ventriloquism of some of the greatest modernist and postmodernist writers is a bracingly original project. And yet one might argue that the "real" Misters Valéry and Henri were an important inspiration for Tavares's growing Neighborhood, and an inspiration, ironically enough, through their own invented characters. Both the eponymous main character of Paul Valéry's only novel, *Monsieur Teste,* a hyper-self-conscious gentleman who attempts to live by the precepts of his intellect, and Henri Michaux's Plume, star of the prose poem collection *A Certain Plume*, have much in common with Tavares's elegant, seemingly befuddled, and yet oddly wise Misters. For example, in one Michaux prose poem, "A Tractable Man," Plume wakes up to discover that the walls of his house have disappeared and, only mildly unsettled, he returns to sleep. When he awakes again, a train is bearing down on him and his wife, but again sleep beckons. Awaking once more, he discovers pieces of his wife left behind by that passing train, but again his eyelids grow heavy. The (sleepy) aplomb with which Plume faces the disasters of the dream and waking worlds reversed reminds me of "Mister Calvino's 1st Dream," where during the course of a thirty-story fall Mister Calvino manages to tie his shoes and knot his tie just before "he touched down on the ground, impeccable." Mister Henri, meanwhile, displays logical leaps that Monsieur Teste might be proud of, in "The Theory," which I quote in full.

> Mister Henri said, "The telephone was invented so that people could speak to each other from far away. The telephone was invented to keep people away from each other. It's just like airplanes. Airplanes were invented so that people could live far away from each other. If neither airplanes nor telephones existed, people would live together.
>
> "This is just a theory, but think about it, my friends. What one needs to do is think at the precise moment in which people least expect it. That is how one surprises them."

Those last two lines might serve as a working definition of Tavares's teasing approach to the reader throughout his work.

Whatever his influences, Gonçalo M. Tavares has carved out an imaginative territory quite unlike that of other Portuguese writers. Yet his literary sensibility remains deeply embedded in his country's culture, particularly the love and respect bestowed upon writers. The identity of poets and writers, contemporary as well as classic, are frequently posed as questions on TV quiz shows. Newspapers and magazines offer as loss leaders collectible coins featuring the faces of authors or limited editions of a poet's latest work. When I lived in Lisbon the most popular television program was the reality show *A Bella e o Mestre*, and three of the four judges were writers. The great twentieth-century poet Fernando Pessoa has posthumously become something of a Portuguese national hero, with new edited editions of his work continually appearing, and his image is available on T-shirts, coffee cups, key chains, notebooks, bookmarks, decorative tiles, even "Do Not Disturb" signs that quote him (one hangs on my bedroom door): "Deus quer, eu durmo, a obra nasce!"—God willing, I sleep, the work is born!

Yet Pessoa is not the only Portuguese writer whose legacy is so lovingly attended. When the surrealist poet and painter Mário Cesariny died in November 2006, every Lisbon newspaper devoted their front page, and the entirety of at least their next six or seven pages, to his life and work. Similar attention observed the passing a few months later of the poet Fiama Hasse Pais Brandão. Throughout Lisbon, streets and parks are named after novelists, poets, and journalists, and statues of the most prominent writers hold central place at popular squares and thoroughfares. Even small towns display statues of local minor poets.

There is a reason for this tradition of admiration, one that has deep cultural and historical roots. A large part of the Portuguese national identity rests on that country's unprecedented feats of exploration in the fifteenth and sixteenth centuries. The great discoveries that created the Portuguese Empire were forged together with the birth of early modern Portuguese literature, not only in the work of Luís de Camões, an explorer himself whose major work, the epic poem *The Lusiads*, celebrated the explorations of Vasco da Gama, but also in the far more skeptical plays of Gil Vicente. While those globe-spanning adventures reside in the distant past, I believe that the Portuguese consider that their writers are continuing the tradition of explorers, though now of a different sort: they are patient discoverers of interior empires.

Small wonder, then, that the Portuguese have embraced the work of Gonçalo M. Tavares, which so often playfully memorializes the mental landscapes of famous writers. An early work, which was published in 2004, around the time of the first books of *The Neighborhood*, is Tavares's *Biblioteca*. This collection of nearly three hundred short prose poems, each one about a different author, from Adolfo Bioy Casares to Zhang Kejiu, employs a tactic similar to the Mister books, by creating a space within which the imagination of the author in question can breathe. These prose poems are like little seeds, with all of the subjects of the Mister series appearing here, while others, such as Mishima, Woolf (finally, a female writer!), and Gogol, are part of the projected expansion of *The Neighborhood*.

Biblioteca reads as a tour through the various strands of influence that have forged Tavares's own work, the essence of his personal library—not the one on the shelves, but the one in his head. And here, I think, is where Tavares, in his growing universe of *The Neighborhood*, connects most deeply with a reader. We each have our own internal library, the jostling within of the various imaginations of the writers we most care for, a library where, as we grow older and the specific details of our favorite books fade, the force of their imaginative universes remains and morphs into a quite personal neighborhood. When we visit Tavares's neighborhood, its building blocks made of books, we are also visiting a version of ourselves.

José Saramago, who once playfully declared he'd like to deck Tavares out of jealousy, has also been quoted as saying, in a much less threatening manner, "Gonçalo M. Tavares burst onto the Portuguese literary scene armed with an utterly original imagination that broke through all the traditional imaginative boundaries. I've predicted that in thirty years' time, if not before, he will win the Nobel Prize and I'm sure my prediction will come true. My only regret is that I won't be there to give him a congratulatory hug."

Well, who knows how to read *those* leaves? We do already know that Saramago won't be there, unfortunately, if that award ceremony comes to pass. If it does, the achievement of the steady population growth of Gonçalo M. Tavares's Neighborhood may very well be a significant factor in his ticket to Stockholm.

Philip Graham
Professor, Creative Writing
Fiction editor, *Ninth Letter*
University of Illinois, Urbana-Champaign
Author of *The Moon, Come to Earth: Dispatches from Lisbon*

The Neighborhood

Mister Valéry

Friends

Mister Valéry was very short, but he used to jump a lot.

He explained: "I am just like any tall person, except for less time."

But this constituted a problem for him.

Later, Mister Valéry began to ponder about the fact that, if tall people were also to jump, he would never match them on a vertical level. And this thought dampened his spirits a bit. One fine day, Mister Valéry ceased to jump. Definitively. However, it was more due to tiredness than for any other reason.

A few days later, he went out into the street with a stool.

He stood on top of it and stayed there, completely still, watching.

"This way, I am just like tall people for a good while. Except I'm immobile."

But he still wasn't satisfied.

"It's just as though tall people were standing on top of a stool and they still manage to move," grumbled Mister Valéry, full of envy, when he returned home shortly thereafter, deeply disappointed, with the stool under his arm.

Mister Valéry then did several calculations and produced some sketches. He first thought about a stool with wheels, and proceeded to draw it.

He then thought of freezing a jump. As though it were possible to suspend the force of gravity, if only for an hour (he did not ask for any more than that), during his perambulations through the city.

And Mister Valéry drew his recurrent dream.

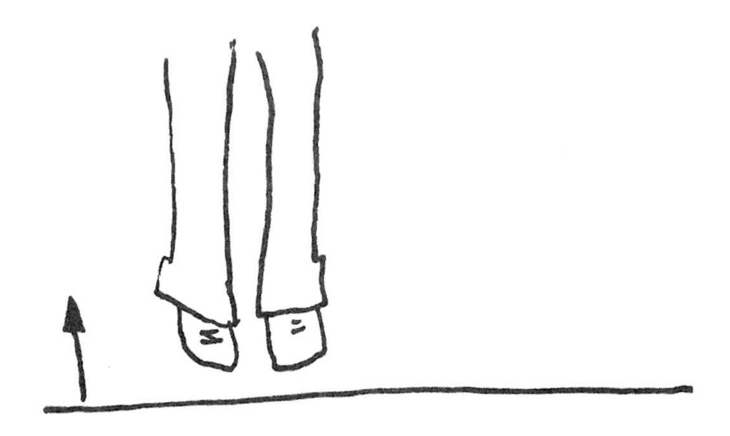

But none of these ideas was either comfortable or possible, and thus Mister Valéry decided to be tall in his mind.

Now, whenever he met people in the street, he looked at them as though he were looking at them from a point that was twenty centimeters higher. By concentrating, Mister Valéry even managed to see the tops of the heads of people who were much taller than he.

Mister Valéry never thought about the hypotheses of the stool or his jumps again, now considering them to be, when viewed from a certain distance, rather ridiculous. However, by concentrating upon his new view of people in this manner, as though from above, he found it hard to recall the faces of the people he met.

Essentially, with his newfound height, Mister Valéry lost friends.

The Pet

Mister Valéry had a pet, but nobody had ever seen it.

Mister Valéry used to keep the animal locked up in a box and never took it out. He fed it through a hole on top of the box and cleaned its droppings via a hole in the bottom of the box.

Mister Valéry explained, "It's better to avoid getting attached to pets, they frequently die, and then one gets very sad."

And Mister Valéry drew a box with two holes: one on top of the box and the other on the bottom.

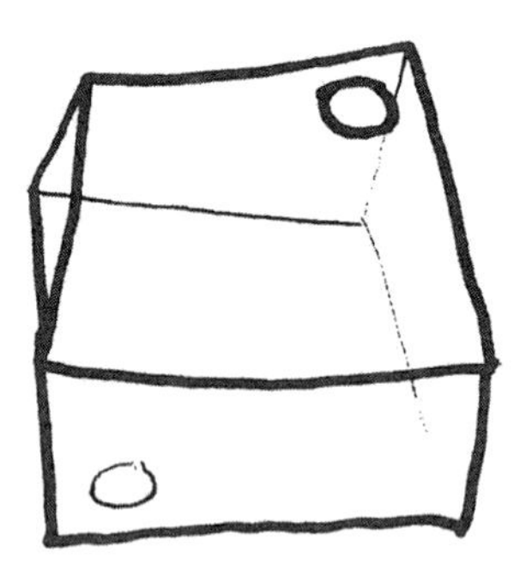

And he said, "Who could get attached to a box?"

Unfettered by any sort of anguish, Mister Valéry thus continued to be very content with the pet he had chosen.

The Hat

Mister Valéry was very absentminded. He did not confuse his wife with his hat, as happened with some people, but did confuse his hat with his hair.

Mister Valéry was under the impression that he always had his hat on, but this wasn't true.

Thinking his hair was his hat, Mister Valéry, whenever he passed a lady, had the habit of slightly raising the hair on his brow, out of courtesy. Inwardly, the women would smile broadly at his absentmindedness, but appreciated the gallantry of the gesture.

Fearing ridicule, Mister Valéry began to be on his guard and, before leaving the house, would jam his bowler hat down to his chin to be absolutely sure that he was wearing it.

Mister Valéry even drew a sketch of his hat and head when viewed from behind

and when viewed from the front.

Mister Valéry jammed his hat onto his head so hard that he could remove it only with great difficulty.

Whenever Mister Valéry met a lady in the street, he tried to raise his hat with both hands, but was unable to do so.

The women continued on their way and, out of the corner of their eyes, could see Mister Valéry sweating away, red in the face with impatience and with one hand on each side of his hat, trying to pull it off his head, rather as one does with the corks of hard-to-open bottles. As they could not wait until Mister Valéry finished his struggle, a performance that sometimes lasted many interminable minutes, the ladies went away before seeing the outcome of the situation.

Thus, Mister Valéry was sometimes deemed to be impolite, which was rather unfair.

The Two Sides

Mister Valéry was a perfectionist.

He only touched things that were on his left with his left hand, and things that were on his right with his right hand.

He said, "The world has two sides: the right side and the left side, just like the human body; and things go wrong when someone touches the right side of the World with the left side of the body, or vice versa."

Scrupulously sticking to this theory, Mister Valéry explained, "I have divided my house into two, with a line."

And drew

"I have delineated a right side and a left side."

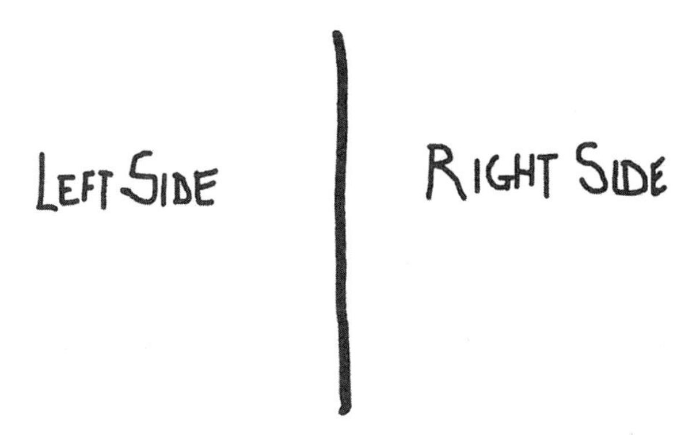

"Thus, I reserve my right hand for the objects on the right side, and vice versa."

At this moment, responding to a question posed by a friend, Mister Valéry explained, "I place any heavy objects with their centers exactly on the line."

And drew

"Thus," explained Mister Valéry, "I can carry them using both my left and right hands, as long as I take care to move them with their centers exactly on the dividing line. In the case of light objects," continued Mister Valéry, "I don't need to worry so much: I change their positions with only one hand. The correct hand, of course."

"But how can you maintain this rigor all the time?" the same friend asked him. "When you are facing the other way, for example, how do you know which is the left and right part of the house?"

Mister Valéry appeared almost offended by this query, as he did not like to be questioned, and replied, brusquely, "I never turn my back on things."

(This was what Mister Valéry used to say, but in truth, so as never to make a mistake, he had painted the entire right side of his house, including all the objects there, red, and the entire left side, blue. Thus, one can better understand the real reason why Mister Valéry had painted his right hand red and his left hand blue. It was not due to aesthetic reasons, as he claimed. It was much more than that.)

The Sneeze

Mister Valéry was afraid of the rain.

For years, he trained diligently to improve his fleetness in order to dodge the raindrops that fell from the sky. He became an expert.

He said, "This is how I avoid the rain."

And, representing himself as an arrow, drew

"Finally," said Mister Valéry, "here I am, completely dry and without an umbrella. I hate unsightly objects," he said.

One day, however, by accident, a lady who was cleaning the pavement threw a bucket full of water onto the road at the precise moment when Mister Valéry was passing by.

Completely drenched, Mister Valéry explained, "I was looking at the sky when it happened."

And added, "If the vertical and the horizontal planes meet there is always a point caught in the middle."

And he then drew

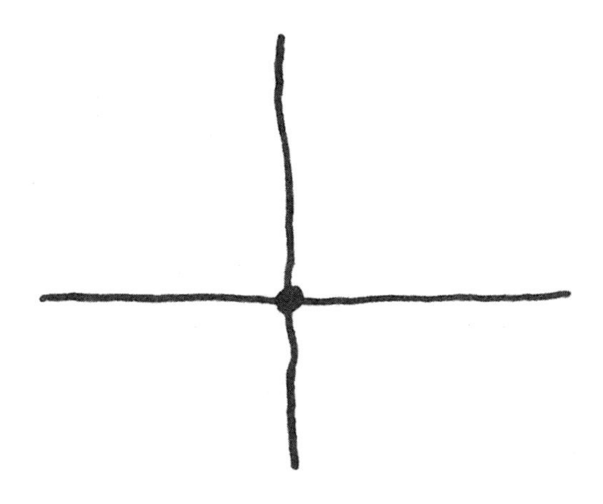

"This point," muttered Mister Valéry, water still dripping from his hair, "this point was me."

"Fate," said Mister Valéry. "I do not know what that is."

And concluded with a loud sneeze.

The Shoes

Mister Valéry used to walk about with a black shoe on his right foot and a white shoe on his left foot.

One day, he was told, "You've switched shoes."

And everyone laughed.

Mister Valéry looked at his feet and, smacking his forehead, exclaimed, "How foolish of me!"

He returned home, changed his shoes, and went out again, later, with a black shoe on his left foot and a white shoe on his right foot.

When they again told him, increasingly amused, "You've switched shoes again!" Mister Valéry grew impatient.

However, remembering the principles of logic that he had learned, he gritted his teeth and while continuing his walk, said to himself, "No. Now they have to be correct."

Mister Valéry explained, "It seems a paradox, but it really is so: if they were on the wrong way, it would be necessary to switch them once again for them to be on the correct way."

And he drew

And then he drew

"One of these two situations has to be correct for the other to be wrong, since they are the inverse of each other. And if they say that the two are wrong it is because the two are right."

After reaching this conclusion, Mister Valéry never worried about whether he was wearing a black shoe on his right foot or on his left foot again. It's always correct, he thought.

The Holiday Home

Mister Valéry had a unidimensional home where he used to spend his holidays. The door and the façade were the only things that existed there.

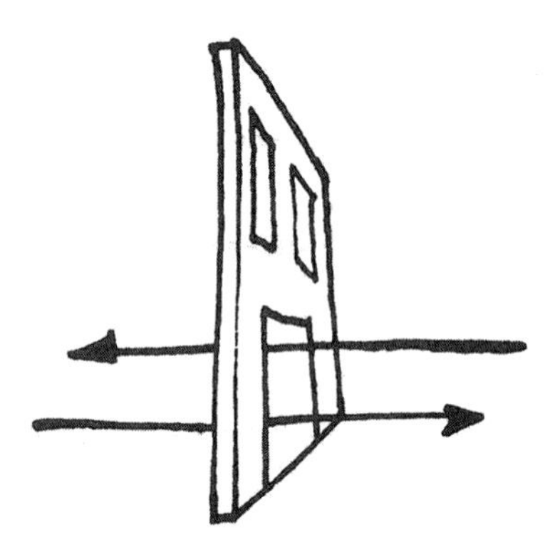

"One can enter and exit in both directions," said Mister Valéry, completely content.

He liked his holiday home.

The only thing better would be a house with four doors, in a square, without any walls.

The center would be the only place where one could be seated.

Mister Valéry drew a sketch.

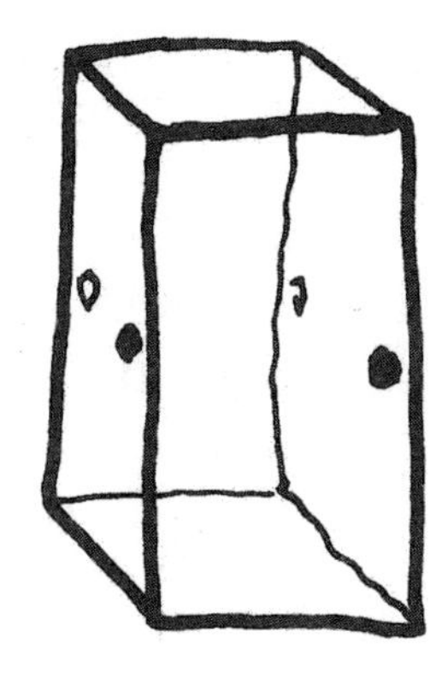

He called it: the house of the four joined doors.

"One can enter from any side and it is always the same. This is the holiday home I would like," said Mister Valéry.

"I would avoid getting lost in rooms," he said. "There would only be doors. It's just that I only manage to rest if I do not have to make any decisions, and for this to happen it is essential that there be no choices. It seems perfectly logical to me."

"This is my dream, this house," murmured Mister Valéry. "It would be a perfect holiday."

The Cube

Mister Valéry always slept standing up so as not to fall asleep.

He explained, "A tower is designed to see everything." And added, "There are no horizontal towers."

However, piqued, Mister Valéry decided to draw a tower on its side.

And he later explained, "If the tower were a cube we would see the same thing, from above, irrespective of whether it was vertical or horizontal."

And he drew a tower in the shape of a cube, horizontally.

He then drew a tower in the shape of a cube, vertically.

"See that? It's the same."

And Mister Valéry concluded by saying, in a philosophical and profound tone, "If all things were cubes, there would be fewer arguments. And there wouldn't be any doubts."

After a brief pause, Mister Valéry added, "I sleep standing up for a good reason."

The Marriage

Mister Valéry was married to an ambiguous being, as he himself used to say.

When Mister Valéry needed something that we can term X, the being was X; and when he needed something that we can term Y, the being was Y.

The marriage worked because Mister Valéry had only two desires.

Mister Valéry explained, "The being I married is like this" (and he drew)

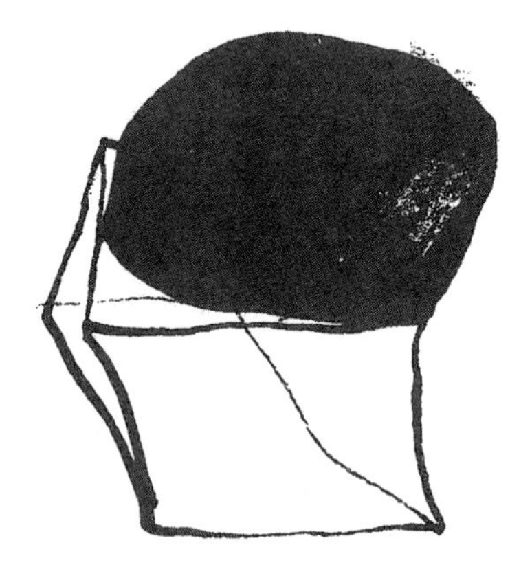

If it were only like this

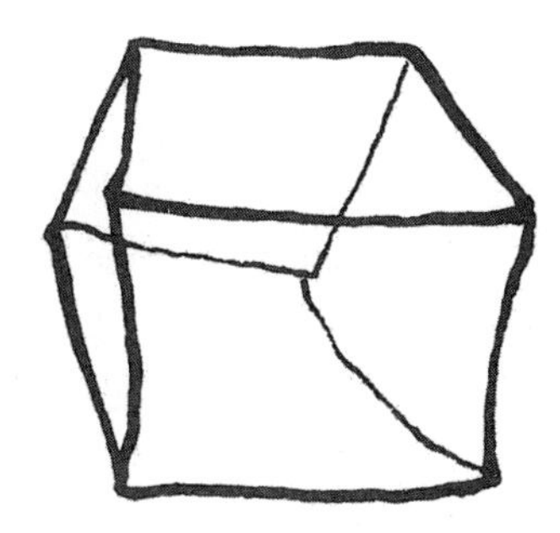

I would grow weary.

And if it were like this

I would get bored.

"Fortunately," said Mister Valéry, "there are imperfect cubes and spheres."

And in a rare play on words, he concluded, ironically, "And that, for me, is perfect."

However, nobody had ever seen Mister Valéry with company.

A Journey on Foot

Mister Valéry walked everywhere. He walked quickly, taking small steps. (In this regard he was like Mr. Sommer, a neighbor).

One day Mister Valéry needed to go to a far-off part of the city.

On foot it would take him ten hours. By train, only twenty minutes.

After pondering deeply, Mister Valéry decided to go on foot. Mister Valéry explained, “Who can guarantee that the place I reach after ten hours is the same one that I reach in twenty minutes?”

And with greater conviction said, “It is obviously not the same place.”

And Mister Valéry then drew two arrows of very different lengths.

And exclaimed, “Only a madman would say that the final point of the two arrows is the same.”

Gaining momentum, Mister Valéry continued, “And even if I went by train and waited at my destination, completely still for nine hours and forty minutes, my destination would not be the same as the one where I would arrive after ten hours on foot;

given that I would have been there, in that place, even though absolutely still, for nine hours and forty minutes, changing it."

And he then began to walk, as he had made his decision.

After having walked for twenty minutes, Mister Valéry looked at his watch and thought, in a somewhat confused manner, "If I were already at my destination, this exact moment would be the place where I would have arrived."

He looked around him and said, "However, this is not yet my destination."

He thus continued walking.

Later, content, still talking to himself, he said, "I still haven't arrived, but the place I am going to is a different one."

And, as he still had nine hours to go before he reached his destination, Mister Valéry continued walking, happy and content with his reasoning, placing one foot in front of the other, always with the same rhythm, heading for his destination.

"Nobody can fool me," murmured Mister Valéry, who was already sweating profusely.

The Problem with Business

Mister Valéry's profession, on alternate days, consisted of buying and selling.

"I sell what I bought on the previous day," explained Mister Valéry, "and the next day I buy something with the money I made from the previous day's sale. And thus, one makes a living," he concluded.

And Mister Valéry explained, "There exists a part on the top and a part below and each sustains the other."

And as he liked to draw, Mister Valéry drew

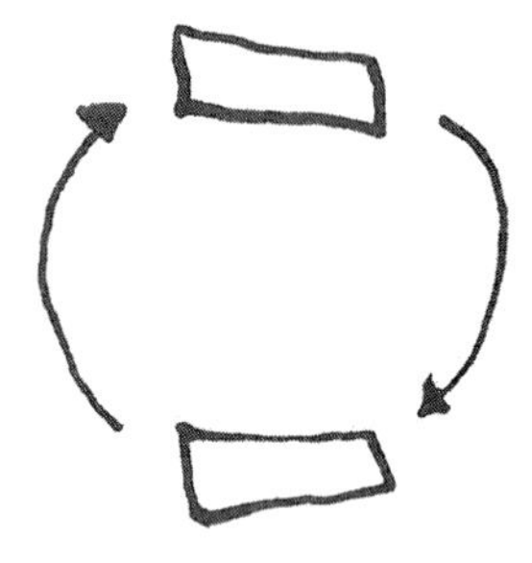

"And it is because one part sustains the other that the circle goes around," added Mister Valéry while he sketched a second drawing.

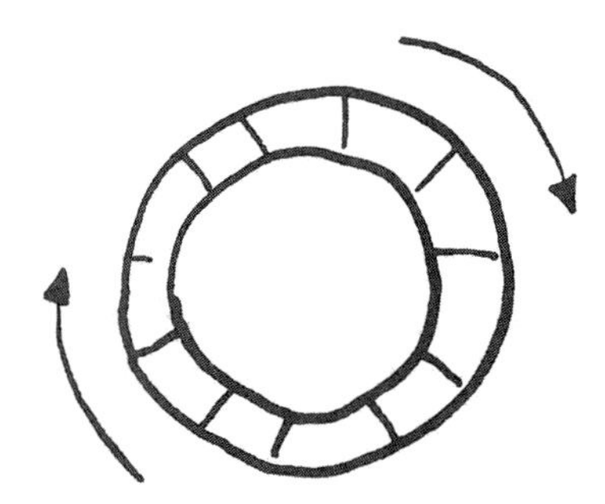

And Mister Valéry made yet another drawing.

"As long as one day follows the other, everything is fine. The problem with this business," whispered Mister Valéry, hoping that nobody would hear him, "the problem is if I were to die. That is the problem."

Laziness

Mister Valéry was sure he was being followed.

"There is something behind me." he said repeatedly.

But he was also sure he was following something.

"I am pursuing something."

He explained, "Everything that exists behind my neck follows me when I move."

And Mister Valéry drew a sketch.

"And I follow everything that exists before my eyes when I move."

And he drew another sketch.

"That is why," concluded Mister Valéry, "I have always preferred laziness."

A Cup of Coffee

Mister Valéry loved his coffee. For Mister Valéry work and drinking coffee were one and the same thing. His work, from a certain point onward, was to drink coffee.

He used to say, "Without my coffee, I can't work," and whoever heard him thought he depended on this substance to do anything else.

But it wasn't so.

Mister Valéry explained, "The human body is so much more exact the fewer tasks it performs."

And further clarified, demonstrating his philosophical ideas of which he was so proud, "A cause is worth less than an effect and an effect is worth less than an event without a cause."

Therefore, he would act without thinking of the effects of his actions. He would act because he liked the action he did. And that was enough for him.

Mister Valéry then decided to draw a cup of coffee in order to prove his theory.

After finishing his sketch, he said to himself, "There are times when I don't understand myself at all."

And as he was confused, Mister Valéry decided to have another cup of coffee.

"It's one way of resolving things," he thought.

The Mirror

Mister Valéry was not handsome. But neither was he ugly.

A long time ago he had decided to substitute his mirrors with landscape paintings. Thus, he did not know what his actual physical appearance was like.

Mister Valéry said, "It's better this way."

And explained, "If I thought I was handsome, I would be scared of losing my looks; and if I thought I was ugly, I would hate beautiful things. This way, I am neither scared, nor do I hate."

And without being either handsome or ugly, Mister Valéry strolled through the city streets, carefully observing the people he met.

He explained, "If they smile at me, I understand that I am handsome. If they look the other way, I understand that I am ugly."

Theorizing, he further added, "My looks are constantly up-dated by the faces of other people."

Sometimes, after meeting somebody who looked away, Mister Valéry, having understood, would run a hand through his hair, ar-ranging his locks while he endeavored to find another visage deep within himself, this time a more pleasant one.

In conclusion, Mister Valéry commented, "Mirrors are for egotists."

"And what about a drawing?" they asked him.

"Today, there is no drawing," replied Mister Valéry, and bid everyone farewell with a brusque but polite movement.

Everyone liked Mister Valéry.

The House Key

Coming out of the courthouse, where they had just heard several contradictory versions of the same event, Mister Valéry said:

"The only chance that truth has of surviving is to multiply itself. If there is only one single truth, then lies can be all those billions of possibilities that remain. Thus it would be impossible to discover the truth: a miraculous chance; whereas lies, on the contrary, would always be around us."

And, in order to illustrate what he had just said, Mister Valéry drew a sketch.

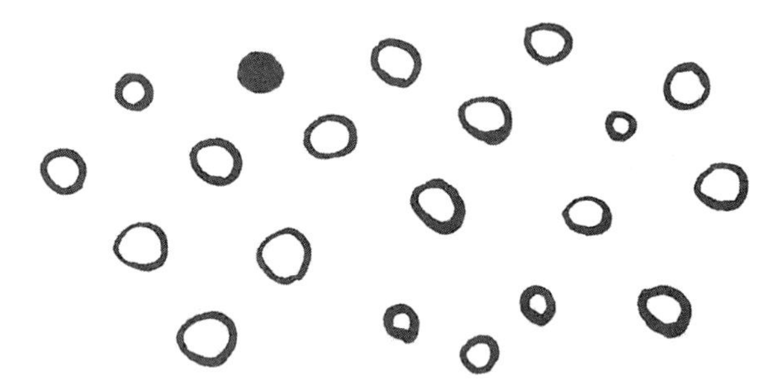

"What we need is to have as many truths as we have lies," said Mister Valéry. (And he drew)

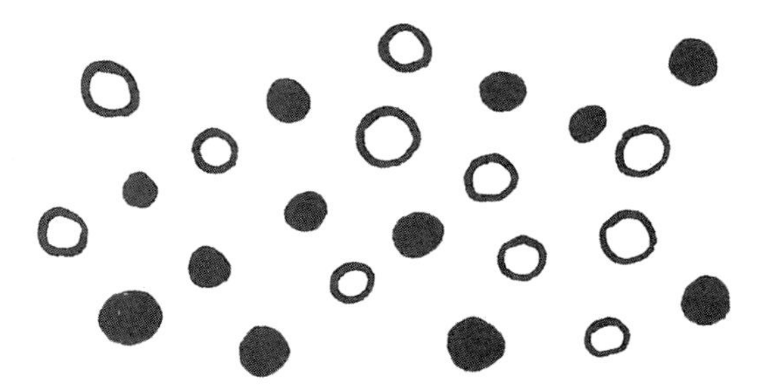

" . . . or even . . ." and Mister Valéry could not help but smile ironically, while he drew

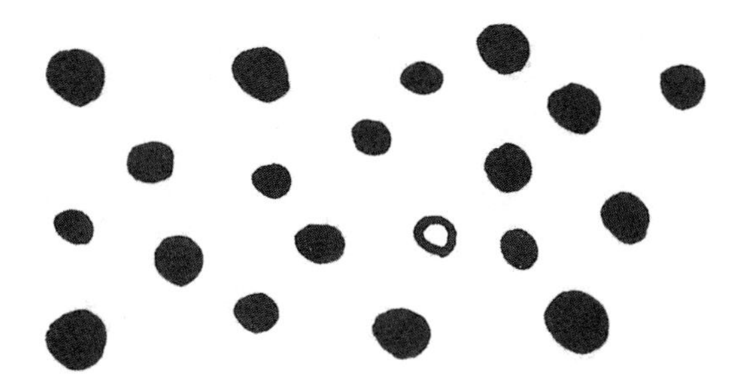

" . . . or even . . ." concluded Mister Valéry, "to have a sole hypothesis for a lie.

Mister Valéry returned home so content with the conclusions he had drawn from this session at the courthouse that it was only when he saw that his keys would not fit the lock that he realized he was standing in front of the wrong house.

"Here we are," murmured Mister Valéry. "If all these houses were mine, with the exception of one, I would probably not have made a mistake. It would really have required a stroke of very bad luck to have erred."

And with this thought in mind, Mister Valéry, without realizing it, once again found himself in front of the wrong door.

"If at least I were rich," muttered Mister Valéry, "I wouldn't worry so much about lies."

And because he had tried to force his key so often into the wrong lock Mister Valéry ended up breaking it, which caused him a great deal of irritation.

Fortunately, he always carried a second key with him. And so as not to make a mistake again, he concentrated his mind totally on the task at hand, thus forgetting, for a few moments, his cogitations.

And this time the door opened.

The Trick

Mister Valéry always wore black. He explained, "When people see me in black, they think I am in mourning and, out of sympathy, don't cause me any more grief."

And further added, "One cannot suffer many things twice over. In fact, some days, that is the only reason why I manage to be happy: my mourning outfit deceives them. And it always feels good to dupe those who are stronger than you," added Mister Valéry, rather proud of himself, though nobody knew to whom exactly he was referring. However, Mister Valéry insisted, "It's like a chemical reaction."

And drew

"If on one side everything is dark and on the other side everything is bright, the dark side tends to offer some darkness to the light side, and the light side tends to offer some clarity to the dark side. After some time, one reaches a state of equilibrium."

(And at this point Mister Valéry drew another sketch.)

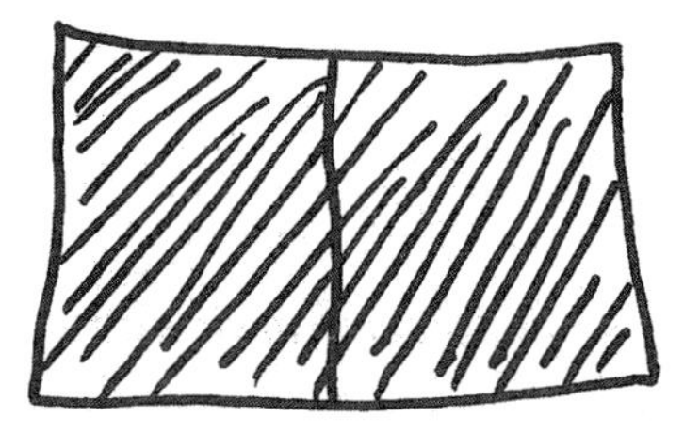

"My trick," said Mister Valéry, while, completely distracted by his reasoning, he put on a white suit, "my trick," he said, "is to always be dressed as though in mourning. To attract happiness."

Three People

Mister Valéry knew only two people. The person that he was, at that precise moment, and the person he had been, in the past.

Mister Valéry used to say, "If I continue to live, I will know a third person."

And at these moments, Mister Valéry would smile, with his habitually vague and intelligent air about him, while, quite satisfied, he walked, with small steps, toward the "Me" that he would meet the following day.

"The past has one Mister Valéry, the present has me, and the future will have another Mister Valéry. By my calculations I am three people. At the very least. However," added Mister Valéry, "three people can be one and the same person if they know each other very well."

And Mister Valéry explained, "If we all ran very fast and the distance was extremely short we could manage to occupy the same space at the same time."

And he drew

"It is possible to run so fast so as to be in all three zones simultaneously," said Mister Valéry, pointing at the sketch he had drawn. "To know three people and to be only one sole person with all of them," muttered Mister Valéry, "deep down inside."

However, Mister Valéry did not have any serious crises of identity, he only suffered from liver problems during winter.

The Nail

Mister Valéry knew arrogant people and did not like them.

For Mister Valéry, an arrogant person was one who thought himself to be above his job, whether this was waiting tables, writing, or painting pictures.

Mister Valéry explained, "I know people who stroll about in the street as though they were doing the act of strolling a favor. It is dangerous to think we are better than our tasks," explained Mister Valéry. "If our job was to knock a nail into the wall . . ." (and he drew)

" . . . and if we think ourselves to be more intelligent than this task, we run the risk of missing the nail, hitting our own finger instead. But we cannot consider ourselves to be less intelligent than the task, as, due to our inhibitions, we again run the risk of missing the nail, and therefore, once again, we would hit our own finger instead. Thus," concluded Mister Valéry, "I consider myself, in any situation, to be at the same level as the task. I am neither its master nor its servant. Me and my task are entities of equal intelligence that during one precise moment have a common Destiny. And that's it."

After this philosophical discourse, Mister Valéry was so happy that he found he was quite out of breath.

The Competition

Mister Valéry did not like competing.

About any kind of competition he would say that every classification was harmful, from first place to the last spot.

And he asked himself, "Why defeat others? Why lose to others? I prefer being vice-last or sub-last," he said, with his usual irony.

And he explained, "A competition can only be fair if everyone has the same conditions. But, as one well knows, this does not exist. And if everyone were equal, how could one individual finish before another? In any competition, people always finish as they began," concluded Mister Valéry.

And Mister Valéry further added, "What I would like to see is a hundred-meter race where each track ended at a different point. Imagine four hundred meter tracks like this . . ." (and he drew)

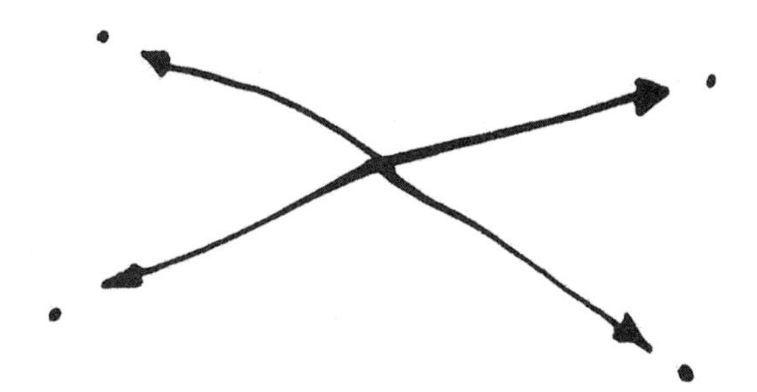

" . . . in this way," continued Mister Valéry, "upon finishing the race, each athlete would better understand what awaited him the following day. Even if he were to win he would end the race alone. Which is a small lesson in life."

And after this somewhat enigmatic statement, Mister Valéry continued on his daily stroll, with his body bent slightly forward, his hat jammed on his head, and alone, completely alone, as always.

The Inside of Things

For several years, Mister Valéry earned a living by selling the inside of things.

Mister Valéry did not sell the object, so to speak, but only the inside of the object. The buyer would take a dish, for example, but in truth he owned only the inside of the dish.

Mister Valéry explained, "This, for example, is a dish." And he drew

"And what I sell is the inside of the dish." And he drew

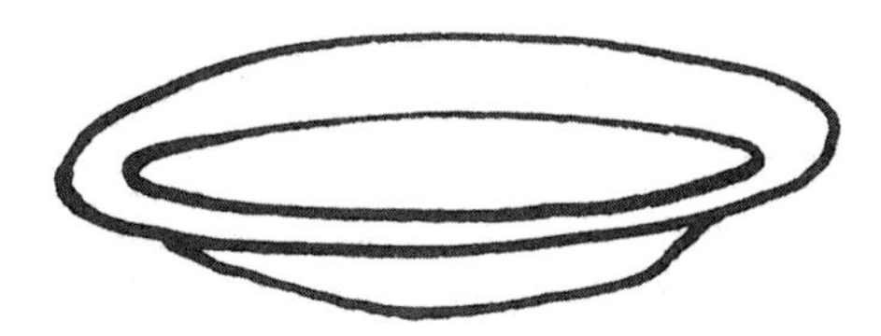

At this point people would say, "But what you have drawn is the outside of the dish!"

"Yes," replied Mister Valéry, "but what I sell is not what you see, it's the inside of the dish. I know it is easier to understand what the inside is in a hollow object," Mister Valéry used to say, "but please do make an effort."

Problems, however, arose when the owner of the inside of

something happened to meet the owner of the outside of that same object.

Heated arguments took place on such occasions.

In truth, both buyers could never be content, unless they lived in the same house. However, such coincidences do not happen very often in life. And that explains why Mister Valéry's business never really took off the ground.

They accused him of being a swindler, but Mister Valéry was merely someone who thought a lot.

Literature and Money

Mister Valéry always carried a book covered in plastic, with a rubber band around it, under his arm.

Besides reading the book, he used it as a wallet, to keep his currency notes.

Mister Valéry explained, "I never liked separating literature from money."

Mister Valéry therefore organized himself thus (these were his rules):

He never placed more than one note between two pages of the book.

He placed lower denomination notes in the front section of the book, and higher denomination notes in the pages at the back.

And instead of using a bookmark to mark the page where he had stopped while reading the book, he kept his coins on that page, thus, in a certain way, making the book look rather plump.

Mister Valéry always kept his identity card on the last page.

This was the drawing Mister Valéry would draw to explain his relationship with literature and money.

And each time he drew the drawing, he would repeat, "I never liked separating literature from money."

Thus Mister Valéry's comportment, both while reading as well as during commercial transactions, followed rigorous and immutable stages.

In the first place, he would carefully remove the book from its plastic cover.

Then, still being extremely careful, so that no coin or note would fall out, he removed the rubber band around the book.

The third step was to open the book to the page where he had stopped reading, which was easy since that was where Mister Valéry kept all his coins.

Irrespective of whether he was engaged in a commercial transaction or whether he was resuming his perusal of the book, Mister Valéry would first tip out all the coins into his hand, holding the book very carefully, so that no notes fell out. Then, if it was necessary to make a payment, Mister Valéry would look for the right notes, leafing through the book like someone who was looking for a particular phrase he had underlined.

If he was opening the book in order to read it, Mister Valéry, after tipping the coins out into his hand, would arrange them in a pile on the table in front of him, and then begin to pay attention to the text. When, in the course of his reading, Mister Valéry reached a page with a note tucked into it, he would immediately move the money a few pages forward.

In contrast, when he was about to finish a book, all the notes inside it, even the large-denomination ones, were shifted to the page behind the one he was reading, that is, the page behind the coins, which always caused him to experience a rather strange sensation.

Whoever passed by Mister Valéry and saw him seated in front of a table in a café, tightly gripping both sides of his book with both hands, was never able to figure out if Mister Valéry's tense arms were due to avarice or a profound love for literature.

Thefts

Mister Valéry had two black bags which he never let go of whenever he was in his two-room house.

He was obsessed with the idea of thieves.

Before Mister Valéry left one room in his house in order to go to the other, he placed all the objects in the room in one of the black bags, and then went to the other half of the house with an easy mind.

When he went back to the first room, he would open the first bag, take out all the objects, and place them back where they belonged, firmly clutching, all the while, the second bag, with all the objects from the other room, in one of his hands.

Mister Valéry explained, "That is why I have so few things. It is very hard work putting them into and taking them out of the bags."

Whenever Mister Valéry went out, he would take both bags with all the objects from both rooms, cross the street, and deposit them in the safe of the Bank.

Mister Valéry explained, "It's only a precaution."

And Mister Valéry really liked drawing his black bags because they were easy to draw.

The Shadow

Mister Valéry did not like his shadow; he thought it was the worst part of himself. Thus, Mister Valéry would go out only after studying the sun at length and verifying that he did not run any risk of having his shadow appear.

Mister Valéry explained, "It's a blot that sometimes becomes visible and foretells death."

And he drew

For this reason, Mister Valéry almost always went out only at night, walking through the unlit streets with a small lantern.

When the city's residents were sitting down to dinner and saw a small light advancing steadily, they knew that Mister Valéry was out there; and, sometimes, on account of the sympathy that this small obsession evoked, they would open their windows and greet him.

"Good evening, Mister Valéry, good evening."

Despite Mister Valéry's diminutive stature, people felt safer knowing that he was somewhere out there, at night, walking through the streets with a lantern.

The Phantom Stepladder

Mister Valéry believed in phantom-objects.

He explained, "Sometimes, on certain nights, right before my very eyes, in my own house, objects appear that I have never seen in my life. They are objects that belong to the people who formerly owned this house, objects that broke or were destroyed. I look at my table and I see a glass on it that I never owned. I glance at the corner of the room and I find a stepladder there that I never bought. Once," explained Mister Valéry, "I tried to climb the phantom stepladder, and I fell down. Quite suddenly, the stepladder simply disappeared. I could have broken a leg but, fortunately, in the meanwhile, a phantom mattress appeared below me and cushioned the fall."

At this point in his explanation, someone asked him to draw a phantom stepladder, and Mister Valéry amiably acquiesced to this request and drew

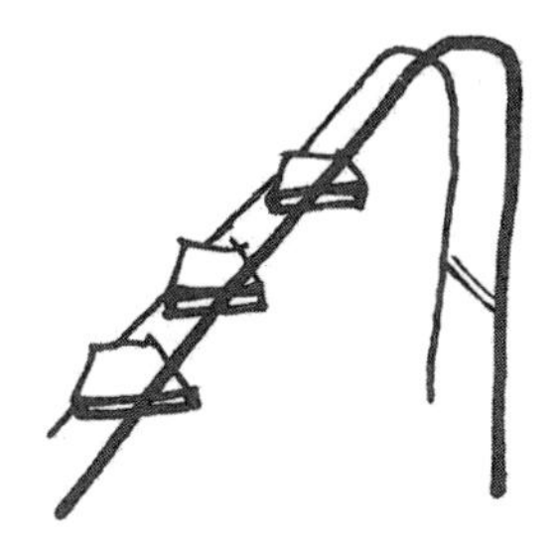

"But that is a stepladder just like any other," they told him.

"It's just like any other stepladder," explained Mister Valéry, "except it cannot be seen."

He then turned his back on these people who irritated him with their remarks, and had already walked a fair distance when, suddenly, he muttered to himself, "They ask me to draw a phantom and then complain about the drawing. That's just how men are."

And with small and rhythmical steps, Mister Valéry continued to walk away from that group of men, step by step, without looking back even once.

Sadness

Mister Valéry always walked along the same streets in the city with the same shoes, one pair for each street.

He had lived there ever since he was born, but knew only five streets, which he walked along with five different pairs of shoes.

Mister Valéry explained, "It's just that I absorb too much. It's as though when I walk down a new street the ground sticks to my shoes and nobody else has space to put their feet. It's as though from then on only birds could traverse the street," he ended, on a poetic note, which was rather rare for him, as he was a man who prided himself on logic.

"The problem," explained Mister Valéry, "does not lie in the shoes, it lies in my desire to take everything I touch home."

And Mister Valéry clarified, "As I do not feel complete just as I am, I think that everything that I am not could complete me, and thus I want it for myself, and I steal it from the rest of the world. In truth, the streets attach themselves to my shoes because I am unhappy," said Mister Valéry, melancholically.

And, recovering his habitual ability for logical reasoning, further added, "If a right-angled triangle were to miss the time when it was a square and wished to be a square once again, it should not attach itself to what it wishes to be (the square), as it will thus never be what it wishes to be."

And after this somewhat confused observation, Mister Valéry found himself obliged to draw a sketch to clarify the idea.

"Well now, look what happens if the right-angled triangle were to attach itself to the shape that it wishes to become, that is, the square." And Mister Valéry drew

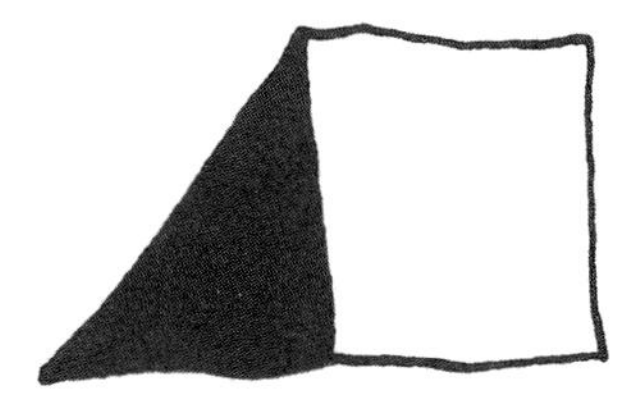

"Essentially," said Mister Valéry, while he drew another sketch, "we should instead attach ourselves to precisely that which we do not like to be, to thus be able to become what we wish to become."

And Mister Valéry drew

"And this is far too confusing, and it's also rather sad," he said, in conclusion.

Mister Valéry did not say anything else after this—he was already tired and it was quite late—however, the last drawing he made was that of a square divided into many small bits.

Mister Calvino

Mister Calvino's First Dream

From over thirty stories above, someone flung Mister Calvino's shoes and tie out of the window. Calvino had no time to think, he was late, he likewise flung himself out of the window in pursuit. While still in the air he reached his shoes. First, the right shoe: he put it on; then the left shoe. In the air, while falling, he tried to find the best position in order to tie his shoelaces. He failed to tie his left shoelace, but he tried again, and this time he succeeded. He looked down, he could already see the ground. First, however, the tie; Calvino was upside down and with a brusque movement his right hand caught his tie in the air and then, with hurried but sure fingers, he twisted it and formed a knot: his tie was in place. He looked at his shoes once again: his shoelaces were firmly tied; he gave the last finishing touches to the knot on his tie, just in time, the moment had come: he touched down on the ground, impeccable.

Mister Calvino's Second Dream

Suddenly, a butterfly. Calvino closed the windows: he didn't want it to be able to get out.

The butterfly settled on his shadow as though it were a surface—a fine black carpet—and not just an illusion.

However, immediately afterward, the butterfly flew off, and settled on the legs of a beautiful woman, who was wearing the skimpiest of skirts; it then flew to the table and settled on the open pages of an algebra book. Calvino watched: the butterfly's tiny feet were on a second-degree equation. Calvino looked at it, at the equation, and then at the butterfly, but the latter flew off again, this time toward the kitchen. Calvino followed it and then froze. There was a raw steak on top of the table, the butterfly circled the meat, but Calvino's hand waved it away in time—certain combinations are unlucky. The butterfly flew out of the room. It first settled on a painting and then flew off again and came near Calvino's left ear.

Calvino felt the colors approach his ear and smiled, he continued to smile while the butterfly entered through his ear, step by step, wing by wing, and went inside his head. Now it was inside and was flapping around his head, its small wings opened and closed delicately and Calvino felt from that moment onward he didn't have to think of anything else, as though the world was, finally, all thought out and resolved, without the need for any human abnegation. Calvino felt happy.

However, still in his dream, Calvino woke up. A strong headache: and it seemed reluctant to go away.

Mister Calvino's Third Dream

He was so involved in a discussion with his partner about the percentages of something that he didn't even notice what had happened: they had been swallowed up by a whale. Inside the whale's stomach, Calvino continued to discuss percentages. He now understood the deal they were discussing, it involved the sale of petroleum and books. Who would get what? The discussion became heated and Calvino got increasingly caught up in it; he then turned his back on his partner and went out into the street: he observed passersby walking from one side to the other. The few that were not in a hurry, the ones who stopped and also discussed percentages among themselves: 30, no, 37!, no, no, 32! Everybody was arguing, Calvino couldn't help but repeat, to himself: 43 percent, at least 43 percent!

But at the same time he had a feeling that they were all inside the belly of a whale and had all been swallowed up a long time ago.

The Balloon

Sometimes Mister Calvino would walk around the city for an entire week, carrying a well-filled balloon with him. He kept up all his normal daily activities, without the slightest change in his routine: his morning walks, the loud and convincing "Good morning!" bestowed upon each person he came across in the neighborhood, the activities necessary for his job, his strictly regulated dinner and his reckless, anything goes lunch, his timetable and punctuality with their classic rigor, his conservative and discreet manner of dressing and smiling, in short, nothing changed—from the moment he got up until he went to bed—except for one thing: between the first finger and thumb of his right hand he firmly clasped, with all the precision of a watchmaker, the string of a well-filled balloon, which he carried with him throughout the day. At work, at home, in the street, at the grocer, where he periodically requested *Apples that are rosier than innocent girls*, at the café, irrespective of whether he was walking slowly or quickly, standing upright or sitting, Mister Calvino never let go of the balloon, perpetually ensuring that it did not burst.

Sometimes, he tied it to his wrist with a string.

At work, when it was essential to have two hands free, he would make a knot with the string around the key to a drawer, and the balloon would stay there, by his side, silent, ever present, and seemingly fulfilling the role, on his table, of the family photographs that some colleagues placed on top of their desks. When nature called, he would go into the bathroom with the balloon and, once inside, would carefully—like someone placing a fragile jar on an unstable base—wrap the string around the doorknob and you could see that he was almost tempted to say, affectionately, just like some people talk to their animals: *Wait a minute*.

While using public transport, during rush hour, Mister Calvino would raise the balloon above his head and would resolutely maintain his arm raised throughout the journey so that a careless movement would not burst the balloon. At home, before going to bed, he would place the balloon near his bedside table and only then would he fall asleep.

For Mister Calvino, paying an uncommon amount of attention (even if only for a few days) to an object like this was a fundamental exercise that allowed him to train his gaze about things in this world. Essentially, the balloon was a simple system of pointing toward Nothing. This system, which was commonly known as a balloon, basically surrounded a minute part of all the air in the world with a fine layer of latex. Without this colorful layer, that air, which had now almost been underlined and singled out from the rest of the atmosphere, would have gone completely unnoticed. For Calvino, choosing the color of the balloon was equivalent to attributing a color to the insignificant. Almost as though he were to decide: today the insignificant will be blue.

And the almost unbearable fragility of the balloon further obliged a set of protective gestures that reminded Calvino of the short distance that exists between the enormous and vigorous life he now had and the enormous and vigorous death that always lurked, like an unseen but noisy insect, around him at any given moment.

The Window

One of Calvino's windows, the one that had a better view of the street, was covered by two curtains that, when they were joined, could be buttoned down the middle. One of the curtains, the one on the right, had buttons and the other curtain had the respective buttonholes.

In order to look out of that window, Calvino first had to unbutton the seven buttons, one by one. Then he would pull aside the curtains with his hands and could look out and observe the world. Finally, after he had finished watching, he would pull the curtains across the window and would button up each of the buttons. It was a window that had to be buttoned.

When he opened the window in the morning, after slowly unbuttoning the buttons, he would feel an erotic intensity in these gestures, like someone who was delicately but eagerly unbuttoning the clothes of a lover.

He would then look out of the window in a different manner. As though the world was not something that was available at any given moment, but was instead something that required him, and his fingers, to carry out a set of meticulous gestures.

The world was not the same through that window.

Alphabet Soup

Mister Calvino carefully wiped off the letters around his mouth with his napkin, but sometimes one letter or another got away. After that lunch, for example, an *A* remained there, stubbornly clinging to the right side of his chin.

Calvino, looking at himself in the mirror, could not help but admire that letter's capacity to tenaciously resist his prior energetic movements with his napkin, and he then observed that *A* like someone who observes a mountain-climber who was desperately clinging on so as not to fall. In fact, that letter seemed to be resisting, and almost instinctively, Calvino thought of that very word—compassion.

That day, Calvino decided to turn a blind eye. Something in that entire scene had moved him profoundly.

And he thus went out into the street fully aware that he had an *A*, a small *A*, on the right side of his chin.

Several people stared at that alphabetical eruption, and Calvino did not fail to notice how some strangers barely managed to restrain themselves from telling him: excuse me, but you have an *A* falling off your chin! But nobody was brave enough to do so.

He had decided he would do nothing to precipitate events: whenever circumstances decreed that the time was ripe, the *A* would fall off his chin. Calvino decided to leave it up to fate and the natural attrition of the world.

Problems and a Solution

Mister Calvino was very tall and his bed did not correspond to his height.

Whenever he slept thus, as in the drawing above, his head was off the bed. He felt that his ideas dripped out from his head, one by one, onto the floor, like a water pot with a hole in it. He would wake up feeling empty, with no initiative.

On the other hand, when he slept like this

his feet stuck out off the bed and he could not get rid of the feeling that he was falling. And the worst part of it was not the feeling that he was falling, but the fact that the ground never seemed to appear. He would wake up extremely tired.

Therefore, Mister Calvino always slept diagonally.

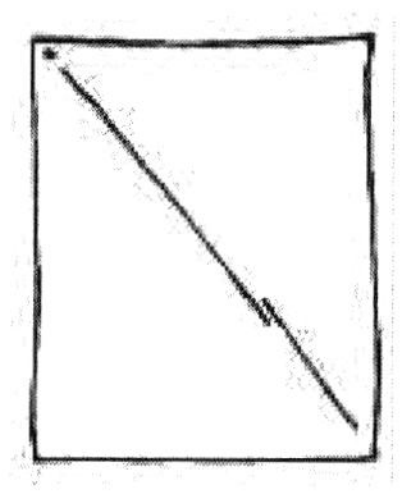

In this way, besides not having any parts of his body outside the bed, he felt he was getting through the night more quickly.

As soon as he fell asleep, he would wake up.

Mister Calvino's Pet

Every morning, Calvino would go to the kitchen to feed Poem. The animal devoured everything: no food was disagreeable or strange—and to him everything seemed to be food.

At the end of the day, after having finished his urgent chores, Mister Calvino would stroke his fur with a delicacy and skillful distraction reminiscent of harpists. During these moments, the universe would spin more slowly, acquiring the intelligent lethargy of small felines.

Giving Poem a bath was not easy; it was almost as though the animal was determined to resist cleanliness, claiming with a bound a shameless freedom that only dirt seemed to allow. But far worse was having to give the animal an injection. It was the only time when his claws were aimed at Calvino. The creature preferred to get sick rather than be medicated.

One day, the animal fell from the second-floor window and died.

The next day Calvino adopted another one.

And gave it the same name.

A Strategic Personality

Calvino described the indefatigable activities of a lazy personality, who felt that being alive was only a pretext to rest, in the following words:

He went backward to the point where he couldn't go back any farther. There was a precipice behind him.

Then he went forward.

But he went forward only up to the point where he once again had space behind him to be able to go backward. He wouldn't go any farther forward. It wasn't necessary.

He went forward just enough to be able to go backward.

Then he once again went backward until the point where he couldn't go back any farther.

He spent days doing this.

Behind him was the precipice. Any farther forward and he would get tired.

He continued like this between here and there.

At night, in order to recover his strength, he would sleep.

He sometimes slept here, and sometimes slept there. But never any farther beyond these points.

Transporting Parallels (Saturday Mornings)

Nobody thought it odd any longer, but they couldn't help but stare.

Every Saturday morning, Mister Calvino would walk from one end of the neighborhood to the other, carrying a single metal rod in his right hand.

However, he did not transport it in just any old fashion. Calvino would carry the metal rod exactly parallel to the ground.

"I am not merely carrying a metal rod," Calvino would say, "I am carrying a metal rod *parallel to the ground*."

This was why he held the rod firmly and precisely in the center and never relaxed his grasp. Whoever saw him leave his house in the morning could note the tension in the muscles of his right arm, a tension that sought to avoid any kind of tremor, and could also admire the way in which he unfailingly carried the metal rod parallel to the ground at any given moment.

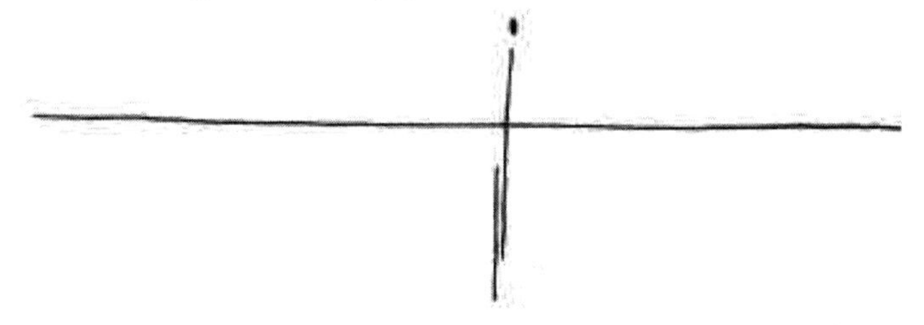

His return trip, however, could not have been more different. Apart from the fact that he held the rod securely in his other hand, the left hand, Calvino now walked in a carefree manner, with his arm completely relaxed, shifting the rod from one side to the other, like someone who was carrying a sack that was of no importance.

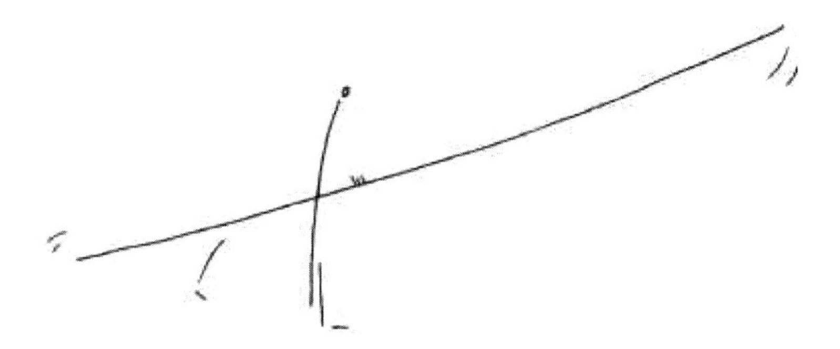

Calvino had explained this right at the beginning and thus nobody was surprised at the abrupt change. If, upon leaving, Mister Calvino ensured that he carried a rod that was parallel to the ground, he brought the very same rod back on his return, but this time held diagonally, which required far less physical effort on his part.

Since the slightest of slips could transform a parallel or a perpendicular into a diagonal, anyone who transported rods that were parallel to the ground of the city was worth his weight in gold; since, above all else, this showed that a person knew how to place his hand precisely at the center of things.

"It's only fair, it's only fair," thought Mister Calvino, while he continued to perfect this specific technical and metaphysical skill every Saturday morning.

Games

Since they hadn't defined the rules, it wasn't very clear:

"We need to define the rules to determine who won, if I did or if you did," said Mister Duchamp to Calvino, once all the pieces had been gathered up and the game had been concluded.

"But now, after we've played?"

"There have to be rules," insisted Mister Duchamp, "so that we know who's won."

"But who's going to define the rules now?" asked Calvino.

"You or me."

"Well, me or you?"

"You can begin," suggested Mister Duchamp, "and then I'll finish."

"No," retorted Calvino. "You begin; each one of us will formulate a rule alternately, and I will define the last one."

"All right. Ten?"

"Ten rules."

They then began, alternately, to formulate rules for the game that they had just played, each one of them trying to define the rules in such a way that, albeit *a posteriori*, one would emerge the victor.

"A study in *Nature* magazine has revealed that the Archaeopteryx, which became extinct some 147 million years ago and is considered to be the link between dinosaurs and feathered vertebrates, could fly like modern-day birds."

So there was nothing new, thought Mister Calvino, putting down his newspaper. Contemporary sparrows and recent eagles flew like the extremely outmoded Archaeopteryx. It was said that they used exactly the same technique. Essentially, they rise up using the air (or keep stable once they reach the desired height) and don't fall. Not falling was part of their nature, and they knew how to maintain it, which is not entirely a disaster. We could say that birds do not forget their essence: they have good memories. Ever since the age of the Archaeopteryx, they have not forgotten that particularly enviable talent of not falling, which is flying.

But one had to admire the excellent memory of the sparrow, who flew exactly like its ancestor the Archaeopteryx, though, on the other hand, one could also criticize a lack of evolution, obviously the outcome of an absence of new ideas. Thus, calling something that flew in exactly the same way as the Archaeopteryx conservative does not seem to be an outrageous insult. Conservative sparrows!, Calvino exclaimed to himself. No new gestures, no unexpected progress in the past few millennia, nothing: in terms of locomotion they stuck firmly to an almost frightening monotony.

Over millions of years, their disdain for the force of gravity—which is an admirable trait—has been expressed in the same way—which has been criticized.

But here is a question that, at first glance, might seem quite absurd: Would modern-day birds know sounds that were unknown to the Archaeopteryx? Would they know new melodies?

This is not, in fact, entirely improbable, thought Mister Calvino, since the modern world was full of new sounds, noises that belonged only to this century or the preceding one: the noise of planes at the moment of take-off or even the noise that we imagine when we see the white streak of a plane that has passed by a while ago in the air; the sounds of typography machines that are so utterly different when they are printing a book of poetry or an essay—as though the machines were well versed in literature!—likewise, the sound when one turns the pages of a twenty-first-century novel, the sound of a Ping-Pong ball escaping four eager but clumsy hands on the floor tiles; the sound of the plastic of a cup that fearlessly falls from a height of three meters and survives, unscathed; or even, for those who paid attention, the sound of the two eyelids of a child who is unsuccessfully trying to master the art of blinking only one eye; in short, thousands of sounds from this century that are undoubtedly heard by the sharp ears of contemporary domestic birds and are then transmitted to wild birds who listen when they pass by a window. Ears that, along with the brain (nothing very refined, but which, despite everything, exists, requires space, functions), ears that then, along with the brain, digest these sounds they hear, and it is no surprise that the sounds they subsequently emit are a result of this digestion, since what is emitted is an effect of what is received—even in birds.

Yes—the contemporary sparrow could say, if it spoke face-to-face with the Archaeopteryx, from 147 million years ago—yes, it's true that I fly in exactly the same way as you, but I—the sparrow would say—I know new songs.

One Morning

Sometimes, obsessed by methods, Calvino would say, “I am interested in the same thing in many different ways.”

At other times, obsessed by things, “I am interested in many different things in the same way.”

Sometimes, confused, “I am interested at the same time in many different ways in many different things.”

Today, upon awaking, lazy, “I am not interested in anything, however I do this in many different ways.”

He didn’t read, he didn’t write, he didn’t think, he didn’t tell stories, he didn’t mentally work out combinations between things: he sat, looked at his shoes, scratched his head, lay down on the sofa—first all curled up, then stretched out, his head first on one side, then on the other, first on his back, then on his tummy—he got up, went to the kitchen, drank a glass of water, looked out of the window, observed the weather, opened the window, put his hand outside, checked how cold it was, felt the wind, closed the window, straightened the key in a drawer, unbuttoned a button on his shirt, walked around the room, and then once again sat down on the sofa.

Some More News

Calvino opened that day's newspaper. He became irritated, but not overly so. It had been clear to him for quite some time now: "This isn't a country, it's a business."

Then he skipped to the last few pages, where he read the following news item:

> Woman Hit by a Small Meteorite
> A 76-year-old-woman was hit by a meteorite (the size of a hazelnut) while in her garden. British scientists believe that the meteorite was part of an asteroid situated between Mars and Jupiter.

"It is interesting to think that the universe, and some of its more distant parts, can have an instinctive flair for mischief, just like a six-year-old child," thought Calvino. Just like some abominable kids throw water from a second-floor window so as to unerringly land on the bald head of an unfortunate passerby, the universe too has its very own old-fashioned catapult and once in while it entertains itself by launching a stone at a septuagenarian who made the mistake of stepping out of her house to take care of the three roses in her garden.

This wasn't malice, nor some intimidatory strategy, it was simply the playful instinct of the universe set in motion. Even a remote asteroid has the right to indulge in sporting pursuits, some would say. The more educated ones.

A Letter from Calvino (on Holiday)

My dear Anna, here the fields, with their robust cereals, continue to conceal sexual movements far better than the sounds that result from these activities. There is thus evidently some discordance between sound and its source. And although this pleasure is a pinnacle above and beyond the subtlest sense of touch, it is nonetheless necessary to highlight the agitated pitch of these sounds that become the main interlocutor in the atmosphere, thus bringing—via the wind—a strong flush to the faces of the village women who thought they would be able to watch from the window, but find that after all they are listening instead.

Due to the fertile fields that serve as curtains, in these moments, where young couples get excited like finely tuned instruments, for a deaf man, my dear Anna, the window suddenly becomes useless.

How to Help Pensioners

"An elderly lady," said Mister Calvino, "a pensioner, who was not agile enough to move forward or backward any quicker, inadvertently got caught in the front door, which had closed thanks to an automatic mechanism that still worked as though it were in the prime of its life. And there was the little old lady, trapped in an uncommonly uncomfortable manner between the inside and the outside of the building. Exactly in the middle.

"And why was she there?" asked Calvino of his interlocutors.

"Simple," continued Calvino, "after several years of not having had any contact with her neighbor, the lady had unexpectedly been invited to tea. At that time, she had been pleased—everyone appreciates a little attention—but now, with the door jammed right between her shoulder blades, she couldn't help but feel disturbed.

"She then thought it rather odd that several days had gone by and the owner of the house had not come to find out what had happened to her. And nobody had gone in or out of that vast property and thus the door stayed the way it was, immobile, pressing her body against the iron beam that functioned as the base of the door.

"After a week she began to feel a pain in her head, more precisely at the base of her neck. The door continued to press down on her bones, which were already rather fragile because of her advanced age. It was quite obvious that no one noticed her absence."

The Spoon

In order to exercise the muscles of his patience, Mister Calvino placed a small coffee spoon beside a huge shovel, a shovel that was usually used in engineering projects. Then, he set himself a nonnegotiable target: a mound of earth (fifty kilos of the world) to be transported from point A to point B—points placed fifteen meters apart.

The huge shovel always remained on the ground, inert but visible. And Calvino used the minuscule coffee spoon to carry out the task of transporting the mound of earth from one point to the other, securing it with all available muscles. When he used the tiny spoon, it was almost as though every little bit of earth was caressed by Mister Calvino's attentive curiosity.

Patiently carrying out the task at hand, without desisting or using the shovel, Calvino felt that he was learning many great things with a tiny spoon.

The Sun

Calvino had a book in his hands whose cover had been almost completely discolored by the sun. What had earlier been a dark green had now been transformed into a soothing, almost transparent green.

He looked at the other books on the shelf. All of them were losing their original color, as though the rays of the sun had chewed or nibbled away—yes, that seemed to be the work of a subtle nibbler—at the book covers.

One book, for example, which had been placed less than a month ago in that corner of the house where, during certain hours of the day, the sun's rays fell directly, now had a rather curious appearance: only one line of the upper part of the book had faded. The rest of the cover on the lower part of the book still retained the brilliance of its original coloring. Due to some unknown association of ideas, Calvino thought of the differences in coloring of areas of the body that were covered or not covered by bathing suits during summer.

He again looked at the shelf and at the faded covers and, suddenly, it was as though everything had become clear: the origin of the phenomenon, the true reasons for the happening that someone would have classified, at first glance, as a chemical happening. But it wasn't as simple as that. Calvino was not merely dealing with a change in substances, this was a force, a strong force that almost had fragile muscles. And this insufficient force originated from the sun: the sun wanted to open the books, it concentrated its rays, with all its might, on the cover of a book because it wanted to open it, it wanted to see the first page, to read, to reflect upon great phrases, to be moved by poems. The sun simply wanted to read, it yearned to do so like a child who was about to enter school.

Calvino meditated. In fact, he could not recall ever having seen a book with its pages open to the sun. It was far more common for people to put down a book on a table or a garden bench (or even on the ground) outdoors, but always, now that Calvino came to think about it, always with the hard cover enclosing the book's contents, denying access to the words inside.

It was thus time for someone to do something. It was time for someone to reciprocate that gentle touch of light that the sun projected on men's faces on certain days, a calm caress, but one that saved men from great tragedy, from despair, sometimes even from suicide.

Calvino once again looked at the books on the shelf that was caressed by the sun. He quickly ran his eye over the spines. With a great deal of attention he chose the most appropriate book; it was obvious that he was not choosing a book in accordance with his own tastes, but instead according to someone else's taste. And finally he picked out a book. "Here's a good first book to start with!" exclaimed Calvino to himself.

He then opened the book to the first page, after the technical details (who would want to read those?), and put the book down like that, opened to the beginning of the narrative, turned toward the point where the sun's rays usually appeared: "Alice was beginning to get very tired of sitting by her sister on the bank, and of having nothing to do."

Tomorrow, he would turn the page again. And over the course of the following days he would continue to do so until the end of the volume.

Mister Calvino Takes a Walk

He sometimes got excited with ideas, not with the world. For Mister Calvino, having a life did not mean merely passing through the turbulent experiences inherent to human closeness and distance. For him, whoever did not have his own thoughts, did not have his own life. Calvino could feel an idea passing through his head just as he could feel the cold on his neck. Of course, this sensation was not tangible like a piece of furniture, it was an ephemeral feeling, but nonetheless an exciting one.

On certain days, his brain got him sufficiently excited, and thus he could avoid other circumstantial emotions. At least those were controllable.

In fact, he clearly remembered the misfortune that had befallen a friend of his. Since his face was paralyzed, this friend always seemed to be laughing, irrespective of what happened.

Mister Calvino suddenly recalled that, according to one historian, a king—whose name was Mahmud—had invaded India seventeen times during a twenty-nine-year reign.

He had taken a vow to invade India every year, but reality does not always conform to the plans of a human heart.

"During a lifetime," thought Calvino, "doing everything seemed to be a lot, and it was impossible to quantify everything and for this very reason it was impossible to verify it. If you couldn't manage it, at least you could try to do half of everything, which had the additional advantage of being an exact number." So, unlike the prognostications of some overly young writers, Calvino decided at that very moment that he wouldn't do everything, he would instead do half of everything.

Well, he had just woken up and, since he did not have any predefined tasks, he had the entire day at his disposal: as though on a platter. To begin with, he would take care of imperfectly describing exactitude. He found it essential to have an initial irregularity, a false step, the inability to understand a part, an expectation created by a surprising fact.

He looked around him.

Nothing. Everything was just as it was meant to be.

He then remembered an absurd dialogue:

"I am sad because I have a sad face."

"And that's the only reason?"

"Yes."

But what was this? Human beings were not so simple. Being sad was not just an official physiognomy (thought Calvino), it was more than that.

The previous afternoon, for example, Calvino had climbed up on a stool.

"Where are you?" asked the blind Mister Bettini, who had gone to visit him.

"On top of a stool," answered Mister Calvino.

At that point, just like someone who was merely inquiring what time it was, Mister Bettini then asked, in his habitually brusque fashion, “From where you are, can you clearly distinguish the Gods from the sheep that are grazing?”

“What?” said Calvino, utterly stupefied.

Why had he remembered this now? He had no idea.

The human memory was not a simple storehouse of old things to which he had the key. Oh well. He proceeded without finding a satisfactory explanation.

In fact, he felt that on certain days he was a rather strange personality.

He saw himself as a pilgrim, but he had no goal and neither did he have a map.

He wanted to go directly to a place where he felt lost, with no detours.

Early in the morning, as though he were talking about the world, Calvino said of the only machine he had at home, “As it is, it never worked, and now it’s got spoiled!”

However, to make up for it, it was almost noon. Time was passing by.

Calvino, it must be added, did not like to stop (to see shop windows?!)—he liked to walk.

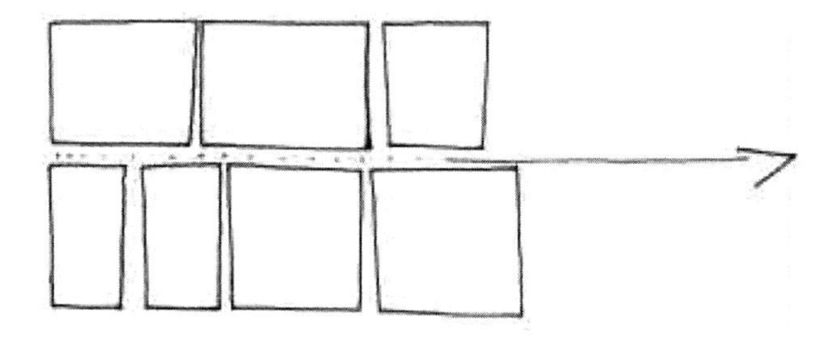

He did not like to accelerate or slow down his pace.

When he was late, he did not speed up. He would simply arrive late.

And he hated waiting. Therefore, when he knew that he was early for a meeting he did not change his route, but instead changed his trajectory within it. He did not stop. He walked down the same street, but in a different way.

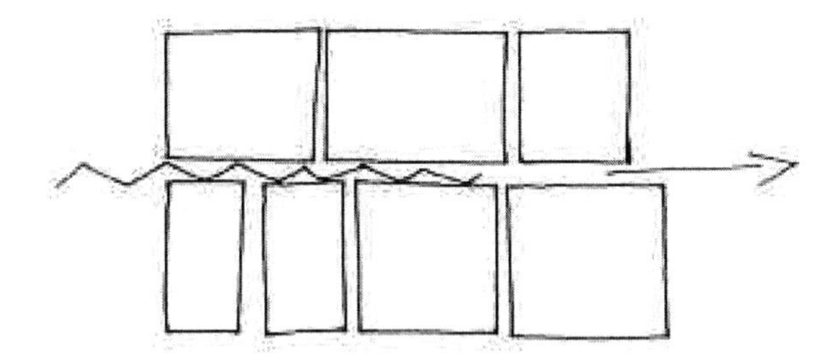

When he was very early, he would do this

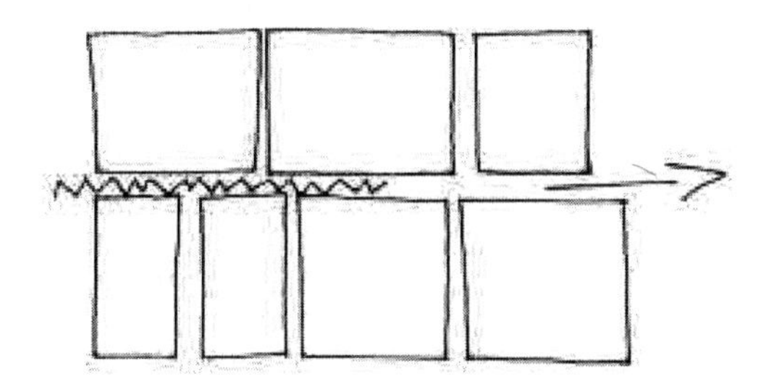

And when he was really very, very early, he would do this

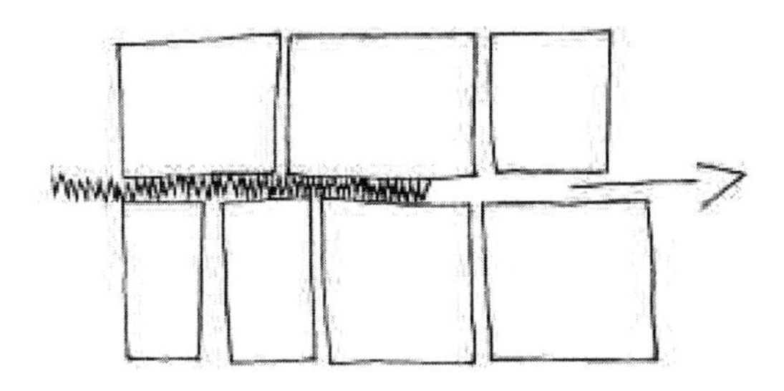

He was now walking down the street at a merry pace, as though the (faceless) muscles in his legs had a millimetric technique of being in a good or bad mood. In fact, his legs were in a good mood, there was just no other way of describing it.

At that moment a pair of lovers walked by him, who, in between nibbling each other's lips and murmuring words less than a centimeter away from each other, were having a great deal of fun in that minuscule space between them, where someone had undoubtedly built an amusement park that was invisible to other people.

Calvino particularly noted the impeccably stupid face of the man in question. "He lacks ideas," he thought, "but for the time being he is not missing them: he's in love."

Subsequently, Calvino's attention was captured by the beating of his heart, as though it were a sort of regular and monotonous music. With his hand on his breast he carefully listened to that wearying music, aware that, after all, this was what allowed him to stay alive. The repetition saved the organism from inside, but on the outside it was indispensable to be prepared for surprises, invasions, defeats, sudden leaps, and other perils.

In a certain way, Calvino did not remember the novelties that were in store for him tomorrow—and this cheered him up immensely. He had forgotten what was going to happen the following day—and this lack of recollection, which is commonly called an inability to predict the future—was a kind of existential reference.

Of course, he never made errors like this:

Buying a (very expensive) ticket, to enter a place where there was no space.

Suddenly, however, he was interrupted. When one is thinking (thought Calvino) one is interrupted as though one was doing nothing at all, people talk to one as though they were talking to an idler:

"Sir . . . where is rue Le Grand?"

Calvino immediately replied, "First right, then second left. Then go up the street till the end and there it is. It's a long walk," he murmured, sympathetically, to the lost man.

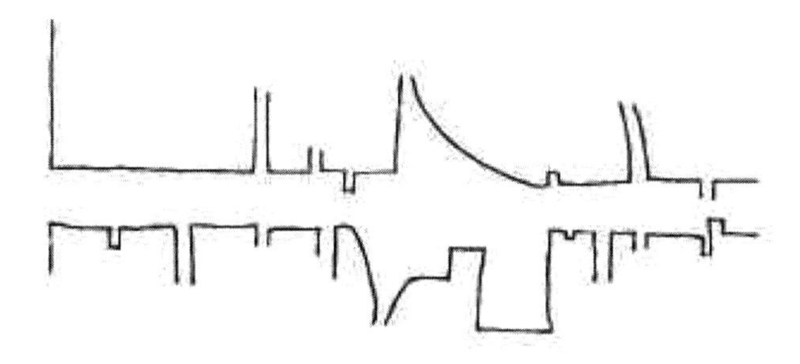

The man thanked him and went away.

Calvino had no idea where rue Le Grand was located.

Calvino did not have enough words to go a day without making things up (some people called this lying). He shrugged his shoulders. It was not a question of revenge, since Calvino was not someone who harbored such feelings. It was simply a reaction to a refined rudeness, this mania that the world had, of disorientingly interrupting, at all hours of the day, those who were lost in their thoughts with requests for clarifications.

"It's just like this, but backward."

This was Calvino's favorite method of enlightening people.

However, he had had no time to enlighten the nice gentleman. It's just as I told you, but backward. He did not feel guilty.

Not at all: to ensure that people got lost in the neighborhood was an act of generous compassion. Just like someone who takes great pleasure in showing people a film or a book they liked, Calvino likewise knew that if people went directly to their destination, without any detours, they would never have the opportunity to see and discover corners that only men who are completely lost discover.

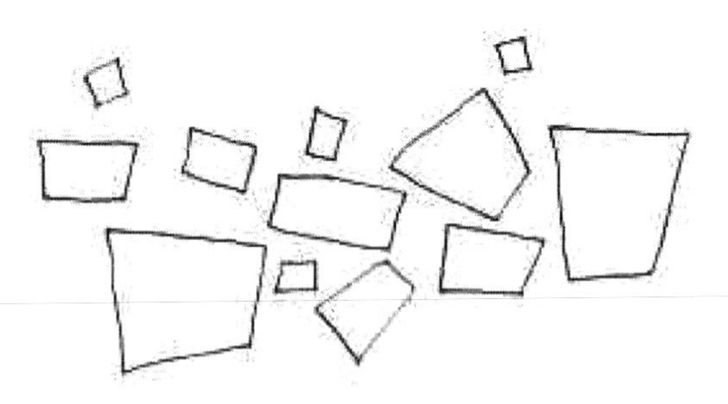

Apart from which, he had known for a long time that it was an intolerant world.

It was possible to spend an entire day telling lies, but it was impossible to spend it telling the truth. All personal and social relationships, and relations between nations, would collapse.

Calvino also knew that a sentence did not have enough space to accommodate the truth; this was not something that could be written or spelled out, but was something that just happened. Like an earthquake or a chance encounter with an old friend at a street corner. Calvino knew that the truth was illiterate.

And there, quite literally, upon turning the corner, was an old friend: the city museum.

Well, since he was in front of the museum, why not go in?

But that was a strange museum.

Anyone who enters a place where musical instruments are on display has the unpleasant sensation of being deaf. Calvino slowly smacked his right ear three times, and then the left one. No, this had to be seen.

There was an exhibition of musical instruments and, in another room, paintings (in glass cases) on display for the blind.

It was as though sensory organs had fallen to the ground and the museum director had mixed up locations and functions while restoring them.

In another hall, photographs of great artists from past centuries were on display.

"A simple calculation," thought Calvino, "would allow us to detect an insoluble enigma: the number of people who were considered to be 'great artists' after they were dead is far greater than the number of people who, in preceding years, when they were still alive, were considered to be 'great artists.'"

The only rational conclusion that can be derived from this is that death is good for art. If all artists were immortal, it is quite likely that we would not yet have a single "great artist."

"It could even be said that it is just as well that they are not immortal," thought Calvino.

A hair in a painting!—how that fascinated him! Just like a cook tends to insistently leave a hirsute hallmark on the product of his art, painters do the same. It was another kind of signature.

This remarkable event—a painter who had left one of his hairs on the painting as though crushed upon the thick paint, an eighteenth-century hair—caused an internal digression in Calvino's mental perambulations that made him think of a children's tale. The story went something like this:

> A princess was brushing the hair of the king, her father, when she found a flea in his locks. The king told her, "Don't kill it, it will grow and could be useful." Well, the flea grew and slowly transformed itself into a prince. The princess fell in love; married him; and when, years later, they began to grow old, she noticed that her husband was now just like her father. The erstwhile prince, who was now the king, had a daughter who, at that precise moment, was brushing his hair. This second-generation princess also found a flea and asked her father, the king, "Do I kill it or do I let it grow?" The king was about to respond, but he was suddenly interrupted by the queen, who yelled at her daughter, "Kill it immediately!"

Yes, a fine answer, thought Calvino: kill it immediately! But if all the world's problems were merely conjugal ones everything would be a lot easier. In fact, the main problem was something quite different.

Above all, it was a question of quantifying the uncontrollable. This was the big question. To quantify what could not be described.

"I do not know how to give names to what I see, but I can do some calculations." This was what Calvino sometimes thought.

Or better still, "I do not know how to give names to the things I see, but I can count them."

Counting, instead of understanding or explaining.

For example, if at that precise moment Calvino was surrounded by various unknown things whose functions and reasons for existing he was unaware of, he could always calm himself down by counting them: one, two, three, four, five, six, seven, eight: eight things that I do not know!

And this reassuringly familiar number, eight, would calm him down. One, two, three . . . eight monsters. “In such situations, at least we have the counting under control,” thought Calvino.

But suddenly, without having been summoned, the world appeared right before him once again. Calvino almost fell over.

On the sidewalk, an iron manhole cover that was not in its usual place had narrowly missed causing him to fall. Calvino stopped and looked inside the hole: various kinds of pipes, in circular or other kinds of trajectories, as though someone had built a sports facility for the water to have fun before it gushed out of taps and became merely useful.

He immediately remembered the relationship that a certain man had with holes.

This man had first looked up and had then looked sideways in both directions, confirming that there was no danger.

Then, completely safe, he let himself fall.

Well, but it wasn’t the right moment to let himself fall.

Calvino then did something that we can describe as seven initiatives to close one single thing.

However, the manhole cover would not fit into the hole that had been made for it. He then amiably handed over the heavy iron cover to a policeman, placing it in his hands, but not without first briefly exchanging a few words with him:

“This is yours.”

“No, it’s yours.”

“Mine? No. It’s yours.”

The discussion with the policeman had, however, left him with a mild albeit persistent pain in his thumb. It had been a mistake to engage in an intellectual discussion with a manhole cover in one’s hands—he would never repeat such an error.

In fact, it was almost as though his thumb had been stricken intellectually. He now moved it forward and backward, then to the right and then to the left, to check if, essentially, some malfunction or rupture had taken place.

It had been man's ability to manipulate his thumb that had enabled human beings to conquer the world—Mister Calvino was well aware of this—but the thumb that could be used against evil also served for detailed amorous trajectories. And this mixture, this confusion between good and evil, pleasure and pain, was far from being the only one in the world.

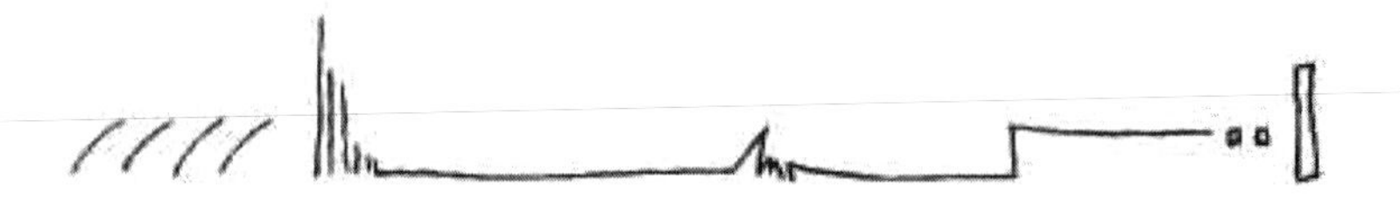

"How do you do, ma'am?"

Mister Calvino was always very courteous. However, that meeting could not help but remind him of a slightly unpleasant story. That of an uncommonly ugly woman who was prevented (at the frontier) from proceeding, since they accused her—and the crime was plain to see—of wanting to traffic in frights.

And since they no longer wanted her in her homeland, the woman in question stayed forever in a no-man's-land, between two nations, a neutral site that tolerated emptiness, tedium, fealty, and other assorted horrors of our civilization more easily.

"Is everything all right, ma'am?"

Calvino had been blessed by an uncommon courteousness. On social occasions, even in strange houses, he would rush to be the first to sit on various chairs. He went successively from one chair to another, while the other guests were still standing—and thus seemed quite ill-mannered. However, what Calvino was doing was trying them—the chairs—so as to later be able to offer the most illustrious individual present the most comfortable and suitable one of all, with the wisdom gleaned from his firsthand experience. Mister Calvino did not try wines, he tried chairs.

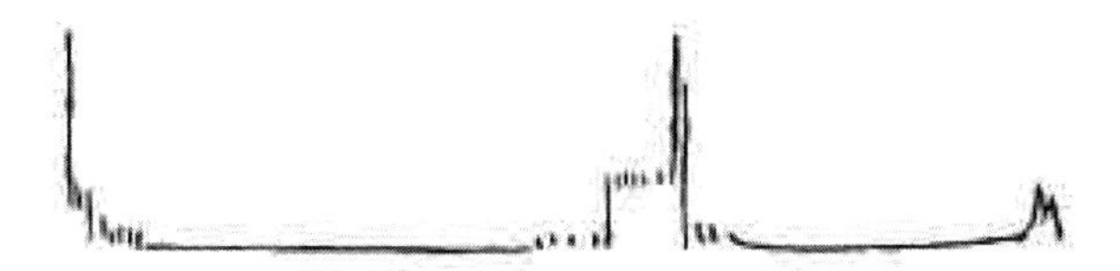

Calvino then cordially bid the lady farewell and a few meters later took a small piece of paper out of his pocket and wrote the following words:

Provincial

—in space

—in time.

An individual who was provincial in terms of space, he ruminated, was someone who was influenced by and tried to influence the forty square meters around himself. An individual who was provincial in terms of time was someone who was influenced by the preceding afternoon and sought to influence, at the very least, the next two days.

In this regard, he recalled that figure described by the writer T., a person who was so cross-eyed that on Wednesdays he was able to simultaneously see two Sundays.

And Calvino thought: yes, that is definitely a lucid gaze.

Well now, having already reached the end of the afternoon, and well inside a narrow street, Calvino first looked to one side and then the other. They were definitely two parallel straight lines, and he, by mere chance and sheer luck, was right in the middle of them.

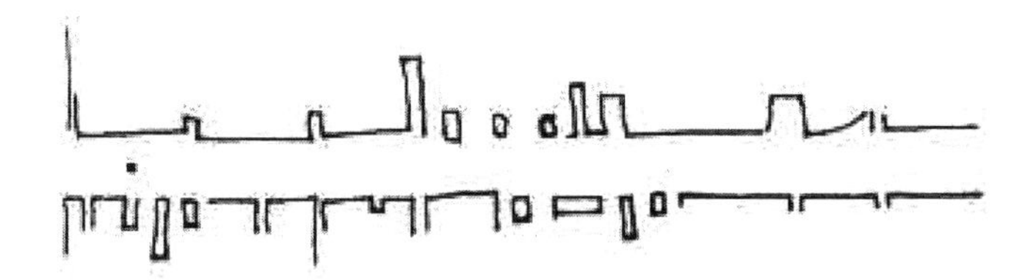

He continued to proceed.

Two perfectly parallel straight lines, and he was right in the middle. What luck. Two parallel straight lines!

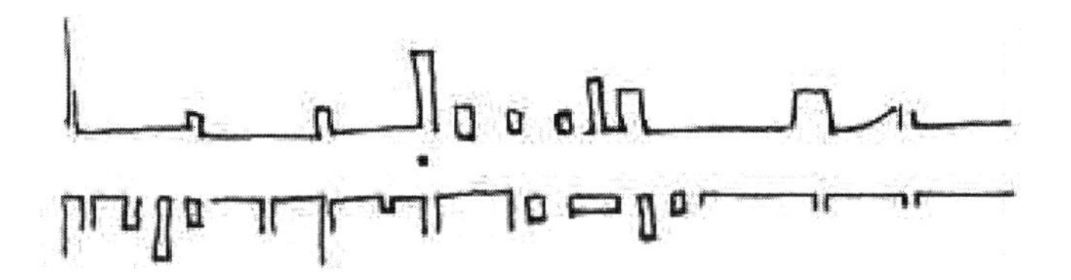

But gradually something began to change . . .

and continued to change . . .

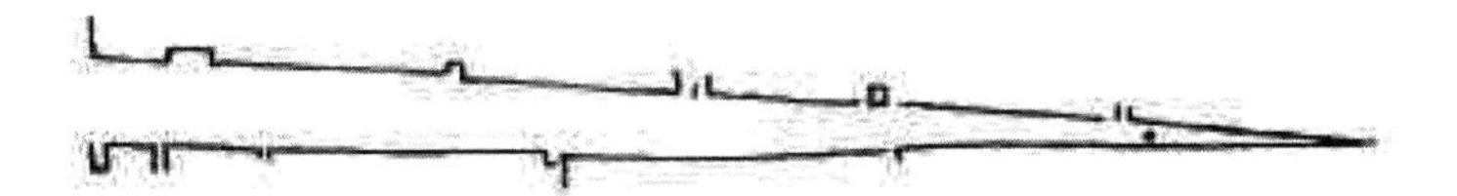

Mister Calvino then stopped (also because he could not proceed any farther).

He had found what so many others had sought: the infinite. He wrote down the address in his notebook.

It was located at the end of Rue de Le grand.

Mister Juarroz

Tedium

Since reality was extremely tedious for Mister Juarroz he stopped thinking only when it was absolutely unavoidable. Situations in which he was obliged to stop thinking included:

—when people spoke to him very loudly
—when people insulted him
—when people pushed him
—when he had to use any useful object around him.

Sometimes, even in these aforementioned situations, Mister Juarroz did not cease to think and therefore other people assumed that:

—he was deaf (because he didn't listen when people spoke to him very loudly)
—he was a coward (because people would insult him and he wouldn't react)
—he was a real coward (because people would push him and he wouldn't react)
—he was clumsy (because things always slipped out of his grasp and would crash to the ground).

However, he was neither deaf, nor a coward, nor was he clumsy. Simply, for Mister Juarroz, reality was a bore.

Dimensions

"Only the left side of a poisonous mushroom is poisonous," thought Mister Juarroz, who, since he had not gone out in a long while, was convinced that reality had only one dimension, like a drawing on a piece of paper. "One can always eat the other side," he would say.

Utility and the Drawer

Mister Juarroz insisted on reserving one drawer in his house in which he could store emptiness.

He even used to utter a very strange phrase: “I want to fill this drawer with emptiness.”

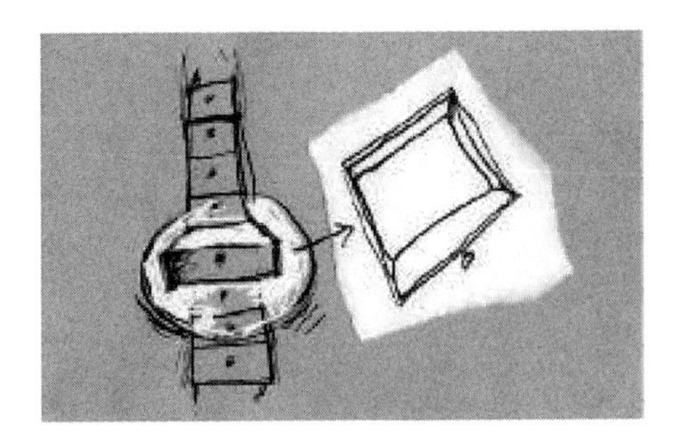

Of course, Mister Juarroz’s wife, who found that she had increasingly little space at home, protested on account of what she felt was a *terrible use of a square meter*.

In order to ensure that his drawer was not occupied by uninteresting objects and transformed into a mere repository, Mister Juarroz would sometimes open it in irritation, showing it to his wife like someone displaying a valuable treasure.

“The drawer is completely empty!” his wife would immediately exclaim.

But Mister Juarroz would shake his head in disagreement. “It’s not yet completely empty. There’s still some space to go.”

“Well, let’s wait another month then,” Mister Juarroz’s wife would murmur, patiently resigned to her fate.

A Theory about Jumps

"The second part of an upward jump is coming down, but the second part of a downward jump isn't jumping up," thought Mister Juarroz.

If you jump up from the ground, you return to the ground, but if you jump down from the thirtieth floor, it's highly unlikely that you'll go back up thirty floors.

In any case, out of sheer laziness, Mister Juarroz always used the elevator.

Falling

"If we keep in mind that falling is a simple shift in location, a change of the body's position along a vertical trajectory, then falls will no longer be so scary," thought Mister Juarroz.

Falling one hundred meters downward and running a hundred meters in the garden, essentially represent the same action, the only difference being the direction of the movement.

"The problem with falls is thus not," thought Mister Juarroz, "a question of the number of meters." From left to right or from right to left everything was all right. From top to bottom was when it became difficult.

"But it's only a question of direction," repeated Mister Juarroz, at the precise moment in which, blissfully unaware of the fact, he once again entered a dead end.

Something on the Roof

Mister Juarroz's wife was beginning to get rather irritated.

"Are you going to climb up or not?!"

Mister Juarroz, however, wasn't paying the slightest attention because he was thinking.

"The invention of the washing machine enabled people to stop washing clothes by hand.

"The invention of the telephone spared people from having to travel long distances only to deliver a message.

"The invention of the stepladder gives people the choice of not having to climb up on it."

Names and Things

To show that he did not submit to the tyranny of words Mister Juarroz would call objects by different names every day.

Thus, half his workday would be spent in attributing names to things.

Sometimes, he would get so tired of this creative task that he would spend the second part of his workday resting.

When he dozed off, the new names he had attributed to things would get mixed up in his dreams with the old names, and sometimes Mister Juarroz would wake up so confused that he would drop the first thing that he tried to hold, and that thing, whose name for a few instants he couldn't for the life of him recall, would break.

A Long Journey

As he liked to read and was setting out on a long journey, Mister Juarroz decided to put six copies of the same book in his suitcase.

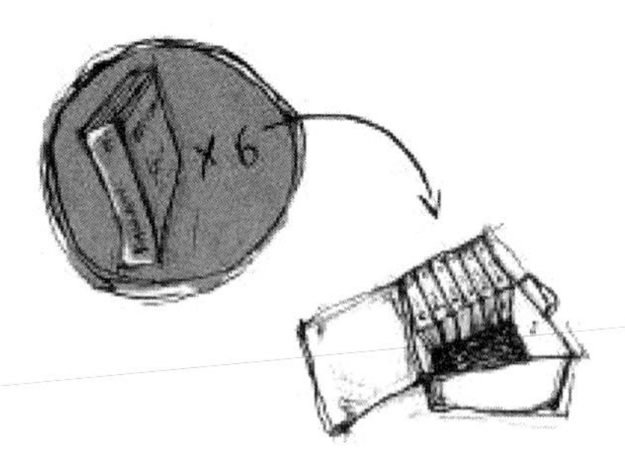

Journeys

But Mister Juarroz's suitcase would be so heavy that he never managed to travel anywhere.

Mister Juarroz came to the conclusion that he could not take his entire house with him when he traveled, because he would not be going to another place but would instead be going toward his own objects. Essentially, he would be going toward his own house. And such a journey would thus be quite unnecessary since, when you come to think about it, Mister Juarroz was already in his own house.

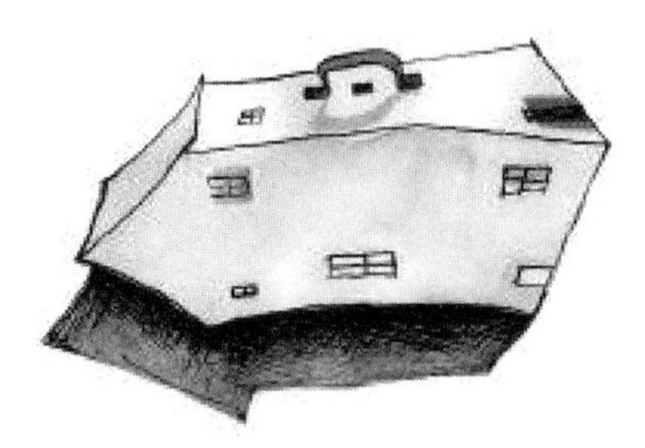

Thus, in order for it to be a serious trip, Mister Juarroz felt he shouldn't take anything with him: not a single item. Bound for the unknown, he murmured.

Just as he was about to leave the house, this time without any baggage whatsoever, he began to think that being thus unprotected he would catch a cold, and starve, besides running the risk of catching various other existential and hygienic ailments.

Therefore, at the last moment, he inevitably decided to stay at home.

Darkness

"The lights! The lights!"

If there was a kind of electricity that could make the darkness appear as there is electricity to make light appear, the number of possibilities would double. But the monthly electricity bill would also double.

"However, it seems to me to be quite unpleasant," thought Mister Juarroz, "that it is enough to switch off the lights to have darkness appear."

In order to give due importance to darkness—at least as much as we give to light—it should be necessary to be able to switch on darkness.

Thus, when the lights are switched off, darkness wouldn't immediately appear but instead there would be some kind of intermediate state.

"Only things that cost money are considered to be important: it thus seems to me to be imperative to be able to switch on the darkness and pay for it," thought Mister Juarroz, a split second before he hit his knee against a table.

"Who switched off the damn lights?!" yelled Mister Juarroz irritatedly.

The Absence of Physical Proof

Since it was quite inelegant not to see anything when there was so much to see, Mister Juarroz stayed at home, glued to the window, watching the world go by.

Since it was possible to hear the silence within the house, Mister Juarroz would open the window to let some noise in for, at heart, he hated silence.

Since hands are, above all, machines to touch things, when Mister Juarroz was at home in front of the open window, he liked to place his left hand against the glass.

Since one of the most endearing characteristics of human beings is their capacity to smell and taste, when Mister Juarroz was at home with the window open to see and hear, with his left hand against the glass in order to touch, he also liked to drink a hot cup of coffee.

Since he liked to think, when Mister Juarroz was at home with the window open, and his left hand against the glass, drinking hot coffee, he would lose himself in his thoughts and, thus, when his wife would ask him what he had seen and heard from the window, Mister Juarroz never knew what to say because he could never remember anything. And only an empty cup of coffee proved something: that he had indeed drunk some coffee.

Mister Juarroz often thought that the world would be more physical if things that were seen or heard would also eventually leave an empty coffee cup, so as to prove to his wife that he was not wasting time, as she accused him of doing. However, even after his bouts of thinking, nothing changed. Since thoughts, too, do not have any proof. Just the coffee, just the coffee—he would murmur.

Shadows

"Of course shadows aren't good for hiding shapes," thought Mister Juarroz, "but they are excellent for hiding colors. But if you hid a white square in a shadow, everyone would make fun of you."

However, just like a diver diving in water, inside a shadow anything that is black and flat disappears.

"For example," thought Mister Juarroz, "a shadow is an excellent place to hide a black square. The only problem is that it is an ephemeral hiding place."

"But there is no hiding place that is not. All hiding places depend on the sun," Mister Juarroz murmured enigmatically.

Shadows and Hiding Places

It's obvious that Mister Juarroz was aware that hiding behind a piece of furniture was not the same as hiding behind a shadow. The problem with the latter was that it lacked volume.

Nevertheless, Mister Juarroz could not help thinking that one could hide better behind the shadow of a high tower than behind the shadow of a lamp. "We're not covered," thought Mister Juarroz, "but we are farther away. And being farther away is another way of hiding."

"However, it's far more tiring," Mister Juarroz would say.

Solving Practical Problems

Mister Juarroz was thinking that the world was completely out of sync, since on the one hand there were floods and on the other people were thirsty, when he finally began to pay attention to the sound of a dripping tap.

Mister Juarroz then spent long minutes observing the drops falling from the tap.

Mister Juarroz then once again began to think that the world was out of sync because there, in his house, there was a tap dripping while that was not the case in other houses.

He then tried to recall which tool was used to tighten the tap and in fact there it was, undoubtedly having been left there by his wife, so that he could do the needful.

The problem was that Mister Juarroz, even after staring at that instrument for ages, could not manage to remember what it was called.

"I don't touch things whose name I don't know," Mister Juarroz murmured to himself, as though he had just established yet another commandment.

He then decided to eliminate the persistent ping-ping of the tap via his thoughts, since he would never manage to do so via his actions.

He began to think of a piece by Mozart, taking great care to ensure that the volume was higher than the volume of reality.

It worked.

The Library

Mister Juarroz liked to organize his library according to a secret method. Nobody likes to reveal closely guarded secrets.

Mister Juarroz first organized his library in alphabetical order according to the titles of each book. However, this method was quickly discovered.

Mister Juarroz then organized his library in alphabetical order, but according to the first word of each book.

It was more difficult, but after a while, somebody said, "I know how it was done!"

Mister Juarroz then reorganized his library, but this time in alphabetical order according to the thousandth word of each book.

There are very persistent people in this world, and one of them, after a lot of investigation, said, "I know how it was done!"

The following day, assuming this round to be the decisive game, Mister Juarroz decided to organize his library according to a complex mathematical progression that involved the alphabetical order of a given word and Gödel's theorem.

Thus, to the amazement of many people, Mister Juarroz's library began to be visited not by bibliophiles, but instead by mathematicians. Some of them spent entire evenings opening the books and reading certain words, using a computer for long calculations, thus trying at all costs to find the mathematical equation that would reveal the system behind the organization of Mister Juarroz's library. Essentially, it was a task aimed at discovering the logic of a series, such as

2 | 9 | 30 | 93

Well, two, three, four months passed by like this, but D-Day arrived. A reputed mathematician, completely red and euphoric, tightly clutching a gigantic pad covered with numerals in his right hand, said, "I know how it was done!" and then presented the formula upon which the organization of the library was based.

Mister Juarroz was disheartened and decided to give up the game.

The next day he asked his wife to organize the library in any way that she liked.

And that's how it happened. Nobody was ever able to discover the logic behind the organization of Mister Juarroz's library.

Two Chairs

Mister Juarroz was ruminating that between one thing and another in this world there was always a space.

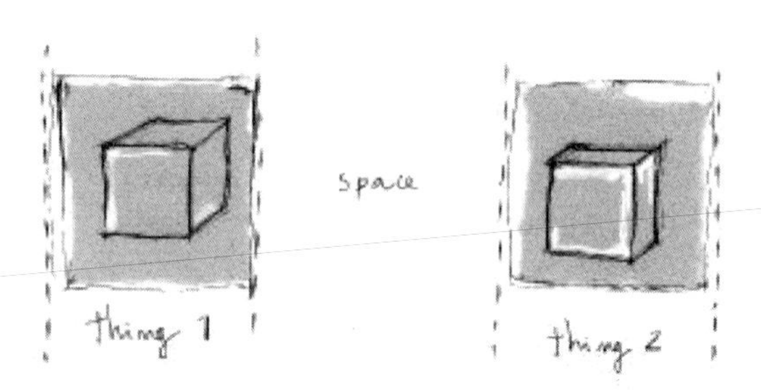

But it was also possible that a single thing could exist

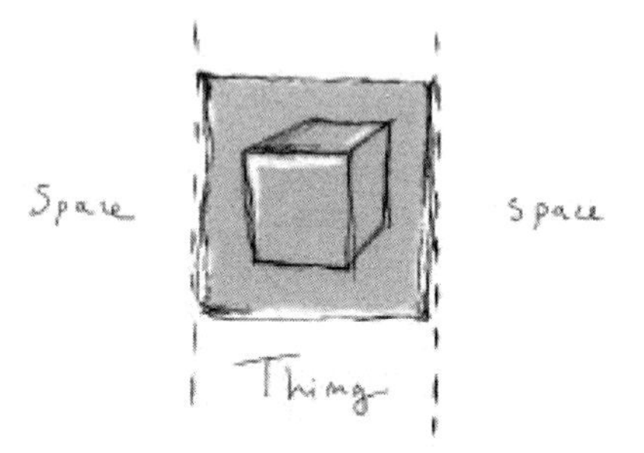

And if this was the case then the spaces became the main thing and the concrete object, endowed with volume and space, became the space (the interruption).

An entire city could be considered to be the space between two empty spaces—said Mister Juarroz out loud, at the precise moment in which he fell on the ground because he had absent-mindedly tried to sit in the empty space between two chairs.

The Organism

"Measuring an organism," thought Mister Juarroz, "is to accept a lie, since an organism, by definition, isn't long, it's hungry. How can you measure something that is changing? How can you measure change?"

The doctor in front of him, however, was about to give up.

"Well, can I weigh you or not?"

"Weigh me only when I finish changing," Mister Juarroz was about to reply. However, he immediately thought that perhaps it was too late at that moment for the medicine to have any effect.

"Please do," said Mister Juarroz, finally, with great finesse.

Manners and Nature

For Mister Juarroz, touching a piece of earth was an obscene act. It was just like peeping through the keyhole of a door and watching a lady undress.

"To touch elements of nature is a lack of manners," Mister Juarroz would say.

In fact, he considered the sense of touch to be the rudest of them all.

Besides betraying a lack of upbringing, touching things also reveals the failure, first of all, of one's thoughts and then of one's hearing and smell and, lastly, of one's sight.

"I touch things only because I have failed," said Mister Juarroz out loud, while he vigorously shook his neighbor's hand.

The Referee

Since Mister Juarroz was not a great sports buff, he chose to compete against himself, via what he called his "two players": his thoughts and his writings.

Thus, he played games to see which was more creative: his thoughts or his writings.

For Mister Juarroz—who considered himself to be the referee in this contest, and therefore detached and neutral with regard to his thoughts and his writings—the same player always emerged victorious: his thoughts. His writings never managed to be as original as his cogitations.

However, Mister Juarroz's decision always caused a great deal of internal turmoil since his writings argued that they had physical and concrete proof of their creativity, unlike his thoughts, which never presented any kind of proof at all. Mister Juarroz's writings always ended up by accusing him of being a partial judge. A cheat, no less.

Cinema

Whenever Mister Juarroz went shopping, he would be so amazed by the shapes and colors of the different products on the shelves that he would reach the checkout counter with an empty basket.

In truth, Mister Juarroz used to go shopping not to buy things but instead to see them.

He didn't go to make material purchases but, rather, visual purchases.

Since they were already accustomed to his ways, the employees of the supermarket, when they saw him enter, would sometimes say, "Mister Juarroz, look, some new products have arrived. They're on the last shelf of that corridor."

And, after thanking them for the information, Mister Juarroz would eagerly hasten his steps in the direction they had indicated.

Finding the Light

Mister Juarroz believed that it was possible to find a point of intense clarity in the middle of the darkest night.

Since he was tired, Mister Juarroz asked his wife to make the following drawing.

Mister Juarroz then prepared himself to go look for this luminous point in the middle of the darkest night.

"And if you trip?" asked his wife.

"I'll take a flashlight," replied Mister Juarroz.

Manual Labor

“For an illiterate person, writing is manual labor,” thought Mister Juarroz. “It’s a physical task just like molding clay or stitching cloth.”

Copying a sentence becomes akin to copying the shape of a vase; and an illiterate person trying to read is like a myopic individual trying to observe someone’s gestures from a hundred meters away.

While Mister Juarroz absentmindedly put his foot in a heap of fresh dung excreted by a rather large animal, he convinced himself, with increasingly elaborate arguments, that everything in life, absolutely everything, was manual labor.

Cups and Hands

Mister Juarroz was always loath to pick up his coffee cup because he couldn't help but think that it wasn't one's hands that picked up objects but rather the objects that picked up one's hands. And this fact displeased him, since he couldn't accept that a simple cup could grab his hand (like an impetuous groom grabbing the timid fingers of a bride).

Thus, instead of picking up his cup, Mister Juarroz would spend long minutes glaring at it aggressively.

Then he would complain that his coffee had grown cold.

The Watch

Mister Juarroz imagined a watch that instead of showing the time would depict space. A watch where the large hand would indicate on a map the exact location where a person was at any given moment.

"And what about the small hand? What would that show?" asked his wife.

"The location of God," answered Mister Juarroz.

The Death of God

Mister Juarroz imagined a God who, instead of never appearing, would on the contrary appear every day, at all hours, ringing the doorbell.

After meditating at length about this hypothesis, Mister Juarroz decided to disconnect the power supply.

Concentration

Mister Juarroz would sometimes wear a blindfold so as not to be distracted by the shapes and colors of things.

When, apart from existing, things also made sounds, to support his blindfold Mister Juarroz would stuff cotton in his ears.

Nevertheless, some things, owing to their strong smell, insisted on infiltrating Mister Juarroz's nose, which would sometimes induce him to close his nostrils with a clothespin.

Thus, with his eyes, nose, and ears blocked, Mister Juarroz could think to his heart's content, without any outside interference.

Before completely immersing himself in his thoughts, Mister Juarroz would also state, to those who wished to listen:

"Now then, please, don't come near me. Above all, don't touch me. Don't spoil everything."

And with his blindfold around his eyes, cotton stuffed in his ears, and a clothespin on his nose, Mister Juarroz, taking great care to keep his hands in the air so as not to touch anything, then had moments of pure ruminative bliss.

How I love this world, he would murmur.

Mister Henri

Literature owes much more
to absinthe than you would think
In terms of quality, even more
than to ink . . .

Alexandre O'Neill

Statistics

Mister Henri said, “Statistics were invented in London in 1662. Before this, random probabilities and recurrences did exist, but nobody noticed them.”

Mister Henri then scratched his belly with the forefinger of his right hand.

Mister Henri was wearing a pair of black pants that did not reach his shoes.

Mister Henri was wearing a pair of old brown shoes. And, when viewed from below, his shoes did not reach his pants either.

Thus, it was mutual: his pants did not reach his shoes and his shoes did not reach his pants.

"An admirable coincidence," said Mister Henri, while he pondered upon the importance of statistics, which were invented in London in 1662.

Philosophers

Mister Henri was struggling with two heavy shopping baskets. They were full of bottles.

Mister Henri stopped for an instant, exhausted, and began to think while leaning against a tree.

Mister Henri said, “They made baskets as early as the Neolithic Age.”

After that, Mister Henri didn’t say anything else because he was very tired.

Mister Henri continued to pant breathlessly, while leaning against a tree.

“I need a glass of absinthe,” gasped Mister Henri.

Mister Henri thought some more and then said, “I now know why one begins to think. It’s due to tiredness. If all men were in good physical shape, there would be no philosophers.”

Before he resumed his stroll, Mister Henri further added, “Fortunately, we have absinthe. Absinthe is the best stimulus for the mind that there is. Sometimes, I really don’t know what thinks better in my head: my brain or the absinthe. But it’s probably the absinthe,” said Mister Henri.

The Neolithic Age

Mister Henri asked for another glass of absinthe.

Mister Henri said, "Today I feel particularly weak.

"They made baskets as early as the Neolithic Age," said Mister Henri. "Baskets!"

And Mister Henri drank the small glass of absinthe in one gulp.

"Baskets in the Neolithic Age! Look at that. In the Neolithic Age!"

Meanwhile, from the other side of the bar, somebody said, caustically, "I'm only interested in things that concern my neighborhood."

And Mister Henri said, "How very sensible of you." And then added, "Another glass of absinthe, please."

The Garden Bench

Mister Henri was in the garden standing before his favorite bench, where a woman was seated, playing the violin.

Mister Henri interrupted the violinist and said, "Antonio Stradivarius was the most famous violin maker of all time. One could say that he was the architect of violins. He experimented with several kinds of violins until he decided upon the size and shape of the Stradivarius violin. I could have been a great violinist, but I never knew how to play the violin. However, alcohol existed well before the violin. Well before violinists existed, there existed people who were artistically inspired by alcohol. Therefore, please get off that bench with your violin. Because that bench is mine," said Mister Henri.

The Mind

Mister Henri was sitting on a bench in the garden wondering if his body would get up in order to drink a glass of absinthe.

Mister Henri said, "My soul has already arisen."

Mister Henri then looked at his body, trying to find his face, but was unable to do so. "There are parts of my body that I can see only with my eyes, and there are other parts that I can see only with my mind. It's as though my mind had eyes, and that these were older than my other two eyes."

Mister Henri then stopped talking.

And then, after a brief silence, Mister Henri said, "What is certain is that my mind has already drunk a glass of absinthe, and I haven't. At this moment, my mind is more drunk than I am. Well then, I'm going to catch up with it," said Mister Henri.

Mister Henri then got up from the garden bench, quite abruptly.

Finally, a decision. "Absinthe, here I come!" he shouted.

And began to walk very quickly.

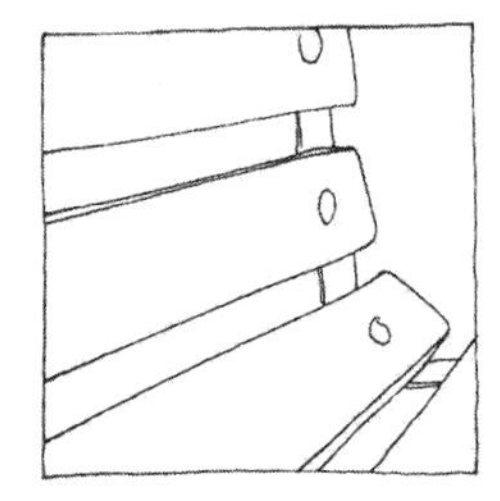

Money

Mister Henri found a ring on the sidewalk.

"Ah," said Mister Henri, "perhaps it is made of gold."

Mister Henri then put the ring in his pocket and thought, "It isn't made of gold, it's made of six thousand glasses of absinthe. That's the currency in my world."

And Mister Henri smiled. He had found a rare treasure indeed.

"Here is the first liquid ring in history," said Mister Henri.

Doctors' Explanations

Mister Henri habitually felt breathless twice a week.

Some weeks this would happen on Tuesday and on Saturday. Other weeks on Tuesday and Friday.

"No air here," Mister Henri would say, placing his hands around his throat.

While he served him a glass of absinthe, the owner of the establishment said, "One of your ancestors must have been hung from a tall tree, about six meters high and a meter and a half in diameter. This terrible event happened on a Tuesday and therefore you are always breathless on Tuesdays."

Mister Henri nodded in agreement and said, "I never liked the doctor's explanation either."

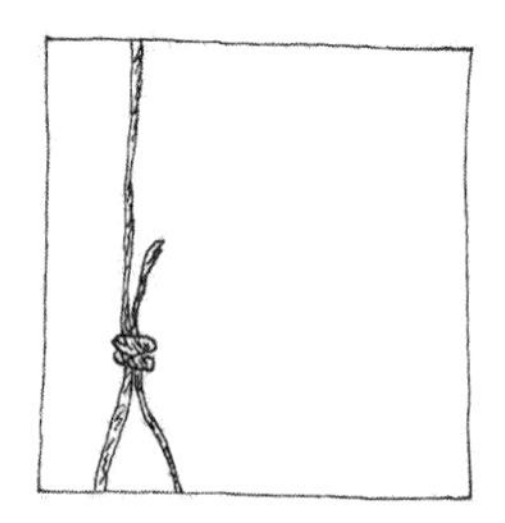

The Eclipse

Mister Henri looked at the eclipse that had been announced but hadn't yet begun.

"If the stars are late, what can one expect of everything else?" said Mister Henri.

Mister Henri had brought along an enormous pair of binoculars.

"If my binoculars were long enough to span the distance between the Earth and the sun, then yes, I would see things from far closer," said Mister Henri.

"In Chinese, they use the same word for an eclipse and the verb 'to eat.' An eclipse is something dark that eats a star. It's a lovely image."

In the meanwhile, Mister Henri put his binoculars down and extracted a bottle of absinthe from his knapsack. After gulping down a few large drafts, Mister Henri said, "What a beautiful eclipse!" And proceeded to quaff a few more gulps of absinthe.

Lying down on the ground waiting for something to happen in the sky, Mister Henri ended up closing his eyes and falling asleep. When he woke up, he grabbed his knapsack and his bottle of absinthe and left.

"I had a private eclipse," said Mister Henri to himself, extremely content with the stars that he had seen in his own private sky. "An eclipse that depends only on me, that is what I have here in this bottle," said Mister Henri.

Earthquakes

Mister Henri said, "If you wish to dig a well, it would be better to first find an anthill.

"Another glass of absinthe," he said.

"Everyone knows that there is always a lot of water under anthills. Ants are therefore plants that are half intelligent and half morons, while plants are animals without any intelligence whatsoever. Ants need water to constitute a family. And in this regard they are just like men.

"Below the Earth's surface there are movements of energy that are symmetrical to the movements that can be seen within an anthill. And earthquakes happen precisely due to a vast quantity of these movements. I read the encyclopedia every day in order to glean these indispensable bits of information," said Mister Henri.

"A man cannot live without information. It's impossible. Information," said Mister Henri, already slurring his words slightly, "information is the other face of absinthe."

Poetry

After drinking a glass of absinthe that he was holding in his right hand in one straight gulp, Mister Henri said, "Another glass of absinthe. It's for both sides of my body," he said. "This glass is for my left hand."

And, holding it in his left hand, he drank the contents of the second glass.

"It's something that is fundamental for a man's equilibrium," said Mister Henri.

"Two is a balanced number. Along with its multiples. Another glass of absinthe, please, let us progress to the multiples!

"In ancient times there existed two forms of mathematics and now only one form exists," added Mister Henri.

"This happened just as it always happens when two peoples go to war against each other and one side wins and the other loses. If people A, who won, are evil, they chop off the heads of all the elements of people B, and then people B disappear forever from the face of the Earth. This was what happened with one of the forms of mathematics. The question is whether the defeated form of mathematics was perhaps more intelligent than this form," said Mister Henri.

"It so happens that very often the losers are more intelligent. One definitely knows that the losers are weaker, as a matter of fact, this is precisely why they are defeated. But just imagine that the people with mathematics A, this mathematics that now complicates our lives . . . imagine that the people with mathematics

A used longer spears than the people who studied mathematics B. Thus, as the tips of the spears of the people with mathematics A pierced the hearts of the people with mathematics B earlier, mathematics A was imposed upon all the peoples of the world. Hence, could one not affirm that the mathematics we use today won by the force of brawn and arms? I believe that the second mathematics, which was lost in the mists of time, gave rise, in many subtle ways, to poetry," said Mister Henri. "However, this is not an absolute certainty. It's a poetic calculation.

"Another glass of absinthe, please. And be quick about it.

"Would you like me to tell you about the fateful years of 1348 to '50?" asked Mister Henri, already perfectly unbalanced.

"Let us then progress to the first multiple," he said.

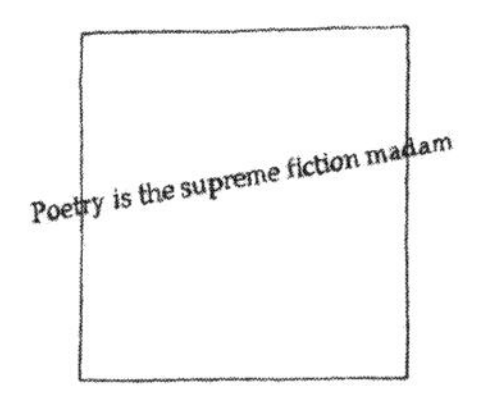

Anatomy

Mister Henri said, "Dr. Joseph-Ignace Guillotin, a distinguished professor of anatomy, invented the guillotine. Dr. Guillotin, the anatomist, said that the guillotine was much quicker than the axe and therefore caused less suffering. With the axe, in the case of some thick-necked assassins, it sometimes took twenty minutes to separate their heads from their bodies. It is necessary to study the human body with a great deal of attention in order to be able to kill people quickly," said Mister Henri.

"Some idiots, like Father Time, take seventy years to kill a person. But it requires a great deal of science to be able to kill in a millisecond. One must therefore conclude that Father Time is not a specialist in human anatomy. Come to think of it, a huge rock smashing down on a skull . . . there are doctors in the most unlikely places, that's what it is."

Bad Luck

Mister Henri said, "Curses are mathematical calculations that happen in the future and wait for us."

Mister Henri bent down to tie a shoelace and, at that precise moment, a huge rock whizzed past his head and smashed on the ground.

"Once again, my luck was timely," said Mister Henri after getting up. "Or rather: my good luck is always synchronized with my bad luck. If a rock were to smash my head, it would be bad luck," said Mister Henri. "But fortunately I was lucky enough to have bent down at the precise moment in which the rock was about to hit my head. People who are unlucky do not cease to be lucky. It's just that they are lucky at the wrong moments," he said. "It's as though they were to find a sack full of sand in the middle of the desert," said Mister Henri.

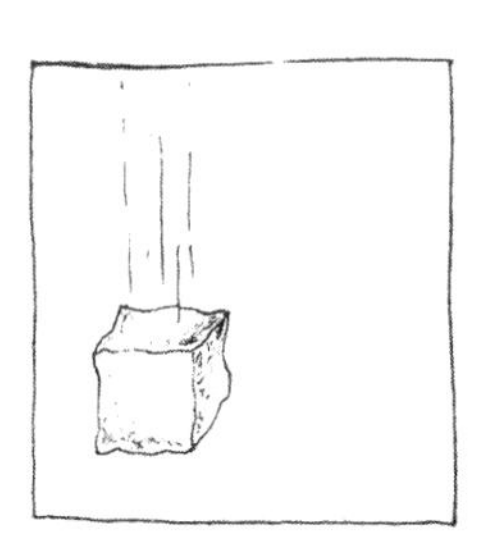

Infinity

Mister Henri asked for a glass of absinthe.

Mister Henri said, “I haven’t drunk a drop for two days now.

“I’ve been measuring an old building,” said Mister Henri,” and if I drink absinthe the measurements of the inside of the house turn out to be almost twice the measurements of the house’s exterior. Is it possible for a house to have a wall that measures ten meters internally and only five meters externally? My notion of infinity is this: a box that measures 20x10x10 on the inside and 10x5x5 on the outside.

“Infinity is contained in absinthe,” he said. And, raising his forefinger, Mister Henri added, “One more infinity please. And make it a large one!”

Influences

Mister Henri said, "Many millennia ago, the Chinese built a tower of happy influences. I read this in the encyclopedia. It was an exceedingly high tower constructed in order to ask, from much closer, the stars to help us mortals down here. If you ask the sun for help with your feet on the ground, the sun can't hear you. The heavens hear giants better than dwarves. It's mathematics. Therefore, when you wish to speak to the heavens, climb the highest tower and shout at the top of your voice. Here," said Mister Henri, "the biggest problem faced by the vocally impaired is, undoubtedly, a lack of voice."

A Lack of Hygiene

Mister Henri said, "The Celts believed that if you made a man deaf, that man would be your slave forever, because he could then not learn anything from anyone else. However, this was during an age when writing had not yet been invented. Nor had cinema. Nowadays it is necessary to make a man deaf and blind and cut off his hands and feet if you wish to make him your slave. It so happens that nowadays one absorbs information from every side of one's body. Which, in my opinion, is an utter lack of hygiene."

The Alphabet

Mister Henri said, “It seems that during the early years of Christianity someone was condemned for having written, ‘the Word entered through Mary’s ear.’”

Mister Henri asked for another glass of absinthe.

“I also know Taoist, Buddhist, and Hindu stories. It’s true that I was never very religious. But if the Church were a giant glass, full of absinthe, it would no longer be a full glass for me. But one must not speak of religion while drinking.

“Did you know that the Babylonians used the same word for ‘pain’ as ‘to eat’? Volume 2 of the encyclopedia, page 376. Instead of, for example, saying that their feet hurt they would say that their feet were eating their bodies.

“I also know things about astronomy and alchemy. I learned about alchemy before I learned about astronomy, because of the alphabet. For me, more important than any historical order is the fact that L comes before S,” said Mister Henri.

The Rainbow

Mister Henri said, "The rainbow was invented in 1656. I'm joking, of course.

"The difference between natural events and human events is that natural events have no date of invention," he said. "Natural events are always far more ancient.

"A glass of absinthe, please," he ordered.

"There are those who believe that nocturnal rainbows also exist, which we cannot see as we are blind.

"And I never really understood progress.

"We drink a glass of absinthe in exactly the same way as the inhabitants of ancient Rome. And they still talk of progress.

"Behold! This is an excellent absinthe.

"Absinthe was invented before intelligence. Now that is one of those rare, incontrovertible facts of history."

Eternal Things

Mister Henri said, "This honorable establishment has had the honor of witnessing some of Mister Henri's most famous speeches, yes, that's me, standing before you, at this very moment.

"Another glass of absinthe, please," he said.

"Today, for example, I am going to talk to you about the microscope. The microscope is an instrument that was invented to make small things greater, while politicians are instruments that were invented to make great things small. The microscope was invented in Holland in 1590.

"In my humble opinion, there should be a date that marks the invention of an instrument and a date that marks the disinvention of that very same instrument. When an invention has been superseded by other events, there should be a burial ceremony, with all the rituals of a grand farewell. Just like with people: a date of birth and a date of death. Rest in peace.

"However, there are some things that are eternal, of course. Things that never die. Things that never lose their value," said Mister Henri.

"Another glass of absinthe please, my dear sir."

And, while he savored his glass of absinthe, Mister Henri added, "Ah! Eternal things."

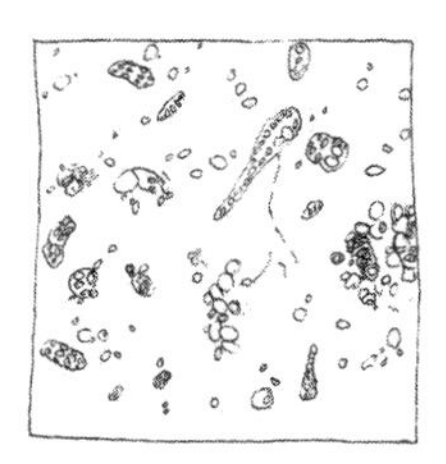

The Two-Stroke Engine

Mister Henri said, "Today, I'm not going to touch a glass. So, by any chance, is there anyone here who would be so obliging as to pour absinthe down my throat? I'm joking," said Mister Henri.

"Half the pleasure of drinking absinthe lies in holding the glass. Well, perhaps half is an exaggeration. I want a glass of absinthe filled to the very brim, and right away," said Mister Henri.

"When I cease to frequent this establishment you, my dear sirs, are going to miss me. I am one of the great financiers of this honorable establishment.

"When viewed in a microscope slide, a king is but a set of worms in thirty different colors," said Mister Henri. "The microscope was the most important invention for democracy. When viewed through a microscope a poor man has as many worms and as many colors as a king. If the microscope had not been invented, democracy would never have been invented. The Greeks were more or less a democracy without the microscope, which, in fact, caused great havoc.

"I've also found out about internal combustion engines. There are two-stroke engines and four-stroke engines. It's exactly like a waltz, except that here—in engines—it's insufferable in one way, while the waltz is insufferable in quite another.

"The only thing that doesn't exist in a two-stroke fashion is death. If death were a two-stroke process, nobody would die because in the interval between the first stroke and the second stroke everyone would run away. Death is a one-stroke engine," said Mister Henri. "Death is an engine that hits one bang on the head in one fell stroke.

"Another glass of absinthe, my dear sir.

"Glasses of absinthe should also be drunk in one stroke. It's a sin to drink a glass of absinthe in two strokes. I thus wish to declare, in the midst of this extremely excellent establishment of drinks and drinks Ltd., that the eleventh commandment is: Thou shalt not drink a glass of absinthe in two strokes. And the twelfth commandment is: And even less so in three strokes. A glass of absinthe should be drunk in one go or shouldn't be drunk at all.

"When one drinks, one does not stutter. That is, while singing and drinking nobody stutters.

"Another glass of absinthe, Your Excellency, because Mister Henri is about to make a toast.

"It's just that Mister Henri is very intelligent," said Mister Henri. "Every inch of Mister Henri's head is crammed with intelligence. Mister Henri has kilometers and kilometers of intelligence inside his head. I have already seen images where his intelligence is all coiled up inside his cranium as though it were a cobra full of perspicacity.

"The question of the two-stroke engine," said Mister Henri, "is that everything that is important doesn't exist in a two-stroke format but rather in a single-stroke version. There aren't two Gods, the one on the right and the one on the left. And there weren't two Great Floods: one at six-fifteen and the other at seven-thirty-five. A fact like that would make the term Great Flood ridiculous.

"All important words are one-stroke ones," said Mister Henri, once again. "For example, the word 'absinthe.' Nobody says:

ab-sinthe. And if they say so, they are sinning against that which is the most sacred of all that is sacred."

And Mister Henri grew silent.

"This long speech has left me rather tired, would the overseer of this establishment be so kind as to bring me another glass of absinthe? Not of ab-sinthe. Of absinthe, always.

"The two-stroke engine is for idiots," further added Mister Henri.

vo-stroke

Reality

Mister Henri said, "If one mixes absinthe with reality, it results in an improved reality. Believe me, my esteemed listeners, when I say that I do not speak from erudition, which I undoubtedly possess in abundance; but no, that's not it. I speak with the voice of experience, my dear compatriots! It is true that if one mixes absinthe with reality, it results in an improved reality. But it is also true that if one mixes absinthe with reality, it results in an inferior absinthe.

"I made the essential choices that one has to make in life a long time ago," said Mister Henri. "I never mix absinthe with reality so as not to worsen the quality of the absinthe.

"Another glass of absinthe, my dear sir. And without a drop of reality, please."

Intelligence

Mister Henri said, "What I dislike about pants pockets or shirt pockets is that they aren't equipped to carry liquids. If items of clothing were better equipped to carry liquids instead of gold, the world would be a much better place. My dear sirs, please do reflect at length upon what Mister Henri is telling you, because Mister Henri is very intelligent. While the majority of people are intelligent from here upward, I am intelligent from here upward and downward. I'm intelligent in every direction," said Mister Henri.

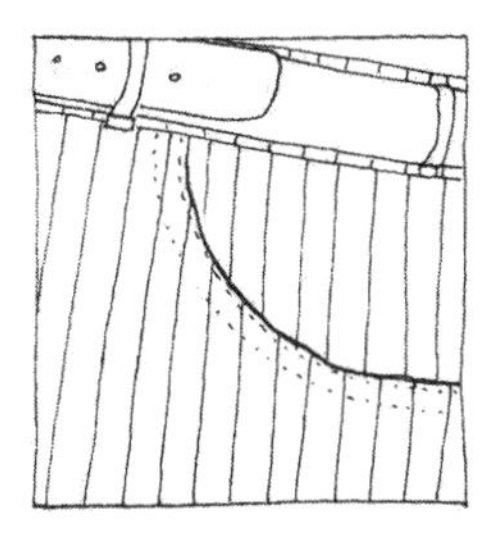

The Part on Top

Mister Henri said, "When I was on my way here I saw a nurse in a garden watering three babies just like one waters plants. And the babies seemed quite happy.

"A glass of absinthe, my dear sir," said Mister Henri.

"If plants are watered by a woman they grow more feminine, if they are watered by a man they grow uglier. I have seen even more astonishing things.

"Another glass of absinthe, my dear sir, because the last one was served in a hurry.

"Studies have proved that intelligence is mainly located in the upper part of absinthe. That is why I always drink from the top of the glass. In truth, I have always been intrigued by the fact that it is not possible to drink liquids from the bottom. But that is not the only mystery in the world," said Mister Henri.

The Contract

Mister Henri said, "My parents never put me to sleep with children's stories. My parents used to put me to sleep by reading me contracts about leases and other things. My father used to work in a notary's office that consisted of a notary and three men who nobody ever noticed. My father was one of them. My father never had time to spend with me and never had time to reread the contracts he was obliged to draw up. My father would make the most of the few moments he had with me before I fell asleep by reading the contracts out loud and would thus check for any errors, and I grew up thinking that children's stories always had two sides, the right side and the left side, two consenting parties, and that one of them gave something in exchange for something else. It was only later that I realized that this really happened in real life—giving and taking—and that it was only in children's books that things were given without wanting anything in exchange. Before he died, my father called me and said, 'Never do anything without first drawing up a contract.' Those were his last words. He was a sensible man.

"Another glass of absinthe! My dear second consenting party. Thank you very much."

The Theory

Mister Henri said, "The telephone was invented so that people could speak to each other from far away. The telephone was invented to keep people away from each other. It's just like airplanes. Airplanes were invented so that people could live far away from each other. If neither airplanes nor telephones existed, people would live together.

"This is just a theory, but think about it, my friends. What one needs to do is think at the precise moment in which people least expect it. That is how one surprises them."

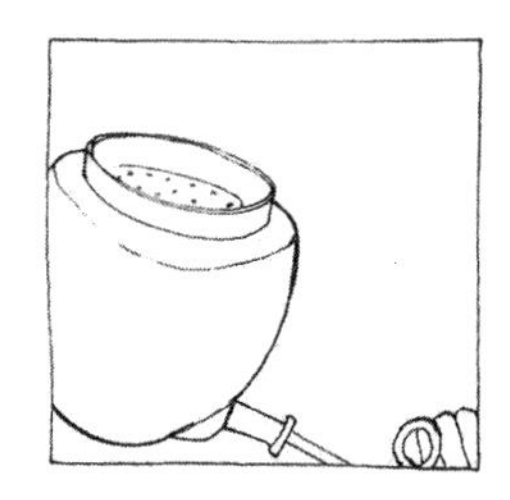

Physiology

Mister Henri said, "The first piano was built in Italy at the beginning of the eighteenth century. From 1880 onward, pianos evolved essentially at the level of structural and tonal capabilities as well as in terms of the speed of traction."

Mister Henri drank a glass of absinthe in one gulp and, immediately afterward, gave a loud belch.

"One needs a great deal of sensitivity in order to play the piano.

"Burping is the language of my forefathers and I beg your pardon for being so attached to my family and for having disturbed you, my dear sirs.

"The advantage of alcohol is that it stirs you up inside. It's a real internal anarchist, alcohol is. Far more effective than revolutionary ideas. Thinking doesn't stir us up internally as much as a glass of absinthe, and all intellectuals should seriously ponder upon this fact. I'm not an intellectual, but I could be one," said Mister Henri.

"If, for every time I drank a glass absinthe in this wonderful library, I had read a book in another sort of library, I would already know the entire history of the Visigoths by heart. The problem is that there are more races than there are cherries in the world, and if I learned the entire history of the Visigoths, I would lose the time I need to study the history of the Ostrogoths, who, by the way, don't exist.

"The best thing to do would be to gather all these facts and events into a book, and then reduce this book to half its size, and so forth, until one managed to condense all the knowledge of this world into a sentence of ten words. Then all of us would learn just that one sentence and we would then have time to seriously enjoy ourselves drinking glasses of absinthe, one after another, just like the Gods recommend.

"In the meanwhile, for quite some time now, I haven't been able to concentrate wholeheartedly on my glasses of absinthe on account of my intellectual needs. I have almost as many intellectual needs as physiological ones.

"If I were to keep an account, in this jar down here, of the number of times that I need to pee urgently, and of the number of times I feel the need to know facts in that jar up there, the total up there would undoubtedly be far greater than the one down here.

"And all this keeping in mind that absinthe tends greatly toward liquidity.

"As strange as it may seem to you, at the end of the year I show a clear deficit in the lower jar. With a greater tendency toward intellectual matters than physiological ones, there is no doubt at all that, in truth, I can include myself in the category of intellectuals. I have more intelligence than physiology, my dear friends. And one only needs to look at your faces for an instant to comprehend that the same is not the case with all of you. I hope you are not offended, but the truth is that your faces, my dear friends, are purely physiological. They're physiology with a nose, that's what your faces are. While my face, if you look closely, is a bit of physiology with a bit of nose, it's true, but, first and foremost, it is a dynamo of intelligence, an animal of profound thoughts, a philosophical industry.

"Just to give you an example: Do you know when the first aircraft carrier was inaugurated? Nothing: it's just physiology. You, my dear sirs, even smell of physiology, which is extremely rare. It was in 1918, nineteen-hundred-and-eighteen. Make a note of that and don't forget it.

"When Mister Henri is no longer here with you, that's when you'll feel his absence, that's right.

"A round of absinthe for everyone. On me. Today I'm feeling particularly happy."

Elegance

Mister Henri said, "The wheelbarrow was invented to give men strength, while women were invented to sap their strength.

"I know I'm a boor, and to compensate for that I'll buy a round of absinthe for every woman present in this extraordinary shrine to viticulture.

"Sir, dear sir, my extremely excellent sir: how is it possible that an establishment like this exists, with this quality of walls and mildew, with this quality of potential diseases due, on the one hand, to a faulty system of plumbing, to the humidity that reigns supreme here, and to the foul and noxious and putrid smell? In short: how is it possible that there is not even one beautiful woman to be found in this realm to compensate for this?

"This may seem to be a grave architectural error, that of not being able to see any women in this establishment; however, one cannot blame architects for all the shortcomings of this world.

"The truth is that the wheelbarrow was invented to give men strength, while women were invented to sap their strength, hence one feels the absence of women because, despite everything, they are the other face of usefulness. In a coin, if you were to find usefulness on one side, you would surely find a woman on the other. Women are the most useless of all man's tools because women are beautiful things.

"But my dear Excellency, the day that a woman should set even one foot in your hall to pay you an extremely excellent visit, I, yes, me, your eternally obliging Mister Henri, in his turn, will not do so: that is, in my turn, not another foot of mine shall ever cross the threshold of this honorable hall to pay you extremely excellent visits! Because women bring worse luck than an empty bottle in the cellar.

"That's what I think. And I beg your pardon if I have offended anyone.

"And this is because women are elegant creatures and elegance is the last quality that has the right to enter these hallowed halls. Every establishment has a mystique, a soul; and the soul of this establishment is to never let elegance set foot in here, I have always maintained.

"And another glass of absinthe, my dear sir, because that was a rather long speech. My throat is drier than a desert between noon and four-thirty in the afternoon.

"Thank you very much, my dear sir, this is what is going to immediately bring me back to the land of the living.

"Here goes."

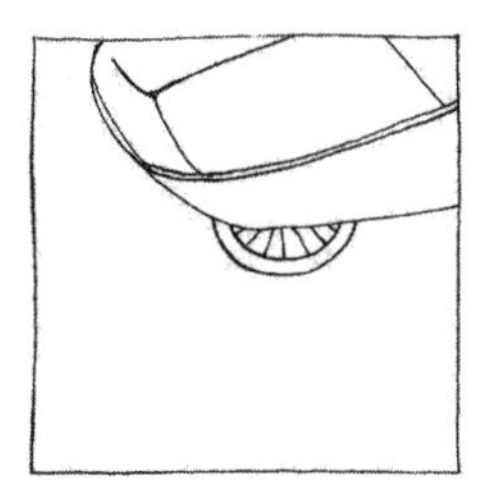

Bones

Mister Henri said, "Steel knives have to be polished regularly in order to get rid of rust. This bit of information may seem insignificant to those who do not have steel knives, but for those who do have steel knives it isn't insignificant at all.

"A glass of absinthe, Your Excellency!

"They say that one doesn't know for sure if the Archimedes' Screw was invented by Archimedes. I always thought that the most important thing was to know how to use the said screw. But if Archimedes' Screw was not invented by Archimedes one needs to change its name immediately. Not another century with errors like this.

"Another absinthe, for pity's sake.

"Our bones belong to us just like the house we've bought," said Mister Henri. "The only difference is that when we don't pay the bank, it isn't so easy to deprive us of our bones as it is for them to deprive us of our homes. The skeleton is the most private of private properties.

"For each glass of absinthe that I drink, I see myself as a gardener watering his garden. My bones need as much absinthe as a garden needs water in summer.

"Another glass of absinthe, my dear sir," said Mister Henri.

"Absinthe makes our bones solid, strong, intelligent, agile, flexible, durable, alert, and, in addition, it's good for our bones. The fact is that bones don't get drunk because drunkenness is always something superficial. One can drink ten glasses of absinthe and your skeleton will not tremble even an inch; what does shake are the nerves around the bones. There are more than a hundred thousand nerves for each bone or some figure like that.

"I've even read a treatise on anatomy where some body parts were missing. I've read a treatise on anatomy where the authors forgot to include both legs and an arm. They went from top to bottom and some things got left behind. A treatise on anatomy that overlooks some body parts is like a summary of the holy Bible on three sheets of paper with twenty-five illustrations.

"For me, absinthe.

"Just so that you, my dear sirs, can understand this, I am going to conjure up an image for you, my dear sirs. For me, absinthe is like a book on anatomy in which no body part is missing. It's like being protected from above and from below and from all other sides as well. So, long live the King, bones, and absinthe! And that seems a rather good summary to me."

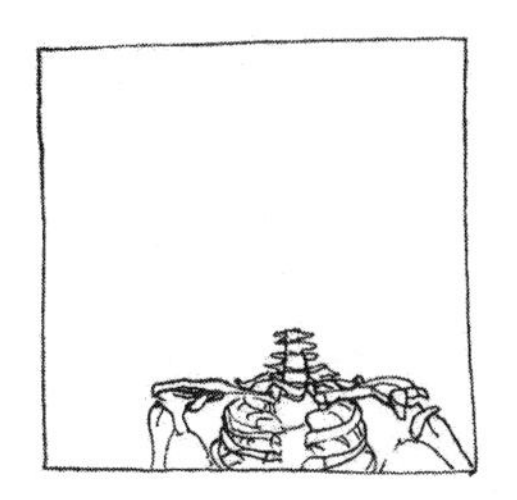

The Sneeze

Mister Henri said, "Flies are forever washing their hands like Pontius Pilate. My dear sirs, do you know who Pontius Pilate was? He was the man who used to wash his hands like a fly. I'm just joking.

"Have you ever observed those flies with their two little paws, always rubbing them against one another? They look just like rich men who have just finished counting their money.

"The main problem of these flies is their level of erudition," said Mister Henri. "Flies do not have a language because they don't have libraries, and if they had libraries they would be erudite. Erudition is a kind of language that is just like ours, except we do not understand it. I am very erudite, but when I step into this library of bottles, I leave erudition at the door.

"This establishment has more flies than Pilate had children. And Pilate, judging by his name, must have had a large number of children. A man with a name like Pilate would impress anyone.

"I know that I am no Pilate, but I have my qualities. And this is the finest variety of humor. The most difficult is to manage sexual humor without wounding sensibilities. One of my qualities is this humor that doesn't wound sensibilities. Wounding sensibilities is a very serious thing. Once sensibilities are wounded, they recover only with a great deal of difficulty.

"And the Lapps believe that a strong sneeze can kill," said Mister Henri. "The Lapps believe that a strong sneeze can kill the person who sneezed, but if they had seen the sneeze that you, my dear sir, just finished sneezing, I think that they would change their opinion. A sneeze like that can kill others. It's just like being hit on the head with somebody's lungs. A sneeze like the one you, my dear sir, just finished sneezing is something that should never be given to anyone. One catches contagious diseases with presents like this.

"My dear sir, you should know that in the Middle Ages a single sneeze could infect an entire village with the plague. My dear sir, we are no longer in the Middle Ages, so you, my dear sir, should no longer sneeze in this manner.

"And, my dear sir, you should also know that, besides being disgusting and spreading diseases, that sneeze is a reflection of a profound lack of courtesy on your part. You should know that it is only out of respect for the honorable proprietor of this establishment that I am not walking out of this reputable establishment. A sneeze like that is worse than a witch's curse. You, my dear sir, should know that this act shows your profound lack of culture and library. A sneeze like that can only come from an uneducated, ignorant person, a parasite on society who chooses reputable places to introduce his powerful poison and thus slowly destroy the solid edifice that constitutes our society.

"My dear sir, I am now going to drink another glass of absinthe to burn all these demons that you, my dear sir, have launched against us with that explosive sneeze, without an iota of pity, just like an executioner from the Middle Ages.

"Did you know, my dear sir, that in the Middle Ages executioners used masks so as not to be recognized later, so that nobody would take revenge? And did you know that in present times executioners no longer need to wear masks, and that they receive a fixed salary from the state? You, my dear sir, should know that this state is the most shameful part of this country, given that it does not protect establishments such as this one, that spread culture throughout our bodies just like a good glass of absinthe does!

"My dear sir, you should know you are a hypocrite, and from now on please don't speak a word to me.

"Please bring me my bill, bartender, and I beg your pardon for my irritability, however, you have some intruders here in your saloon who are not worthy of the noble ground upon which they tread.

"Good evening, my dear sirs, in general, and a bad evening for you, my dear enemy. And do not forget that I am just like an elephant: I never forget, and I shall not rest until I have squashed you. And you should know that elephants have teeth and not horns. Apart from everything else you, my dear sir, are an ignoramus. You, my dear sir, probably know nothing about the characteristics of ants, let alone knowing anything about elephants.

"You, my dear sir, get out of my air space, as you would infect bacteria who were already sick. You, my dear sir, are more poisonous than a family of scorpions and an assembly full of politicians, not necessarily in that order. You, my dear sir, are not even worthy enough to be drinking at all. You, my dear sir, are a mistake by nature, and a tragic error on such a marvelous day, that the Good Lord was kind enough to bless us with. You, my dear sir, harm the sun. You, my dear sir, are worse than an animal. And, my dear sir, stop standing there in silence because it is very unsettling. You, my dear sir, are a beast, and that's all I have to say. A beast, that's what you are. And don't forget your umbrella tomorrow because it's going to rain. You, my dear sir, don't believe in God and you don't know how to drink absinthe. You lose your self-control. And you don't believe in God, as I am well aware. It's a sin, not to know how to drink absinthe properly. Absinthe has to be respected. Not be drunk the way you drink it. You, my dear sir, are an agnostic in every way. I bet that you, my dear sir, are an agnostic even with your wife. I'm just joking. You, my dear sir, wouldn't understand my brand of humor, as you are ignorant, illiterate and an imbecile. And I'll tell you something else, far more serious: you, my dear sir, do not know how to drink. You, my dear sir, do not even know the meaning of the word 'agnostic.' You, my dear sir, get angry, and lose your self-control. See you tomorrow, you are what you are, and goodnight to everyone. You, my dear sir, are a nincompoop. They don't sneeze like that even in China!" said Mister Henri.

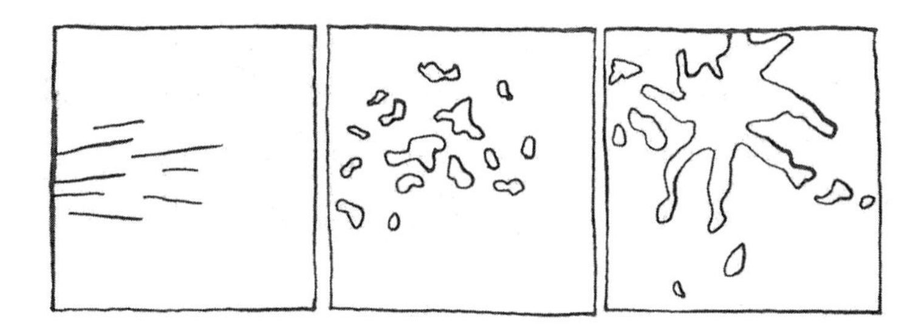

The Bare Essentials

After a prolonged silence, Mister Henri said, "Today I am going to enter and leave without uttering a single word. From today onward, I am going to limit my words to the bare essentials, since I have noticed that my encyclopedic dissertations are not duly appreciated in this establishment.

"From today onward, I shall open my mouth only to ask for more absinthe, and nobody will ever hear me utter another word about anything else because, basically, you, my dear sirs, are a bunch of drunks.

"From today onward, only the bare essentials.

"And with regard to information, I shall stop right here.

"Another glass of absinthe, my dear sir," said Mister Henri.

Mister Kraus

Mister Kraus left the newspaper in a good mood. He knew that in these modern times that were racing by (backward?, sideways?) "the only objective way of commenting about politics was satire." Well, having been hired to write a chronicle that followed major events in the country, Mister Kraus went home, at the end of that afternoon, humming one of those monotonous and repetitive children's songs that, owing to some complicated internal circuitry and associations that were not very clear, had suddenly popped into his head.

Mister Kraus sent his first chronicles to the newspaper.

An Afternoon in the Life of the Boss

1

The Boss was in his office calmly walking from one side to the other at a great pace around his table, entertaining himself by once in a while violently yanking out a hair from his scalp while he simultaneously controlled his bellow of pain, in a kind of game with himself, which he himself classified as "almost fun," when, suddenly, a great deal of confusion broke out, there down below.

For the Boss, in fact, all his vexations inevitably came from "there down below"; it was almost a decree-law.

"I have to eliminate the part down below from the building," thought the Boss, "there's just no other solution."

In fact, horrible shouts were emanating from the habitual source. And they were getting closer.

The Boss squared his shoulders, waiting.

"When danger approaches, commanders face it with squared shoulders and a head held high," thought the Boss. But he immediately bent down to pick up a small coin that had fallen out of his pocket.

He once again squared his shoulders, standing ramrod

straight, stiff, with his head held high, as though there was no other coin in the world on the floor. Completely vertical, this was a Man.

Meanwhile, the shouts began to take shape.

They then acquired the worst shape of all: they were the voices of his Assistants. They never left him alone.

The Boss was tired of despairing with the help of those men. He had the right to despair alone, like a real Boss. But there they were again, his Assistants.

2

He locked the door from inside. Later, he could always say that he had been in an important meeting.

If he was the Boss, and hence the apex of authority, wasn't it important to think by himself for himself?

In fact, he could manage to have by far the most important meeting of all on his own.

In order to sound more convincing, when he would justify the locked door, he began to talk to himself, as though he were arguing with one of his earlier thoughts.

As he was not used to not agreeing with himself, the first words that he uttered were, "Bravo! An excellent idea!"

3

By now the assistants were quite close.

They ran about shouting, frightened.

Something serious had happened.

The Boss stood straight, raised his arm and pointed heavenward with his forefinger.

He liked this gesture; he felt as though he were showing the people the path to follow.

Except that there was nothing above his office. Only empty halls. And some toilets.

"Upstairs, you need to go upstairs," the Boss seemed to say, with that gesture involving a raised arm and his forefinger stretching skyward.

And since he had been unable to get the people out of his head in the past few minutes, he felt moved and amazed with himself.

He, who before becoming the Boss had never, but never ever, thought of the people, was now completely immersed in thoughts about them, about the people (whom he had never met).

"This can be learned," he murmured. Like a new high-jumping technique; it can be learned.

But they were already there, on the other side of the door, knocking on the door leading to his office.

"The Economists!"

"The Economists are on their way!!" yelled the Assistants, anxiously, from the other side of the door.

4

"What's the hubbub all about?" asked the Boss. "I was despairing, but calm. What have you now come here to . . ."

"The economists say that it's necessary to reduce expenses even more!" said the Assistants in unison, breathlessly.

"What expenses?"

"Other people's expenses!"

"Ah, other people's expenses!" exclaimed the Boss, relieved.

"Yes, Boss, but we can't let our guard down. Because when the economists" (and this word was uttered as though the thought of repeating it out loud sent shivers down their spine) "say that it is imperative to cut other people's expenses they keep looking at us. Staring, in fact."

"At us?!" exclaimed the Boss, indignantly. "But we aren't other people!"

Suddenly everyone fell silent, all at the same time, almost as though it had been planned beforehand.

The Boss was nervous.

He straightened his tie and lightly tapped the belt holding up his pants.

The First Assistant immediately also straightened his tie and lightly tapped the belt holding up his pants.

In quick succession, the Second Assistant straightened his tie and tried to lightly tap his belt. But he couldn't: he had forgotten to wear a belt.

He lowered his eyes, ashamed, but the Boss wasn't looking at or listening to anything.

"This thing about the Others," he murmured, "this thing about the Others has always intrigued me."

"Yes, the Others," murmured the First Assistant, unsure of what he should say.

"The Others are fascinating!" exclaimed the Second Assistant, suddenly, as though he had just discovered the answer to an arithmetic question.

"Calm down, Mister Assistant," said the Boss, who was gradually recovering his self-control, "don't exaggerate! The Others are necessary! Necessary! Understand this word well. They are not fascinating, that's something else."

He then opened the window and tried to gradually calm himself down by counting the number of Necessaries that were walking by from one side to the other.

"Necessary!" he repeated out loud, with his back to the Assistants. "Necessary!"

Instinct

The Boss detested geography, economics, literature, chemistry, sociology, engineering, mathematics, physics, and all the sciences invented after Christ. What he appreciated was instinct.

"Instinct, you see!"

The Assistant saw that his Boss did not want him to see. So he shook his head.

"Don't you know what instinct is?"

The Assistant once again shook his head, even harder. He was a good Assistant.

The Boss liked to explain—anything, even the inexplicable—and the Assistants liked the Boss. He didn't have any other opportunity. He thus charged toward the Assistants like a bull, in certain popular ceremonies, charges toward hurt, limping men who get left behind.

"Instinct," said the Boss, completely absorbed in his dissertation, "instinct is something that is born here," and he pointed to his stomach, "and it rises, and rises, and rises," accompanying his words with appropriate gestures," until it reaches here!" and his right hand gripped his own throat. "Here, you see!"

"To your throat!" exclaimed the Assistant, as though a two-thousand-year-old secret had just been revealed to him.

"More than to the throat," specified the Boss (he specified very well), "instinct rises up to my vocabulary and all this is as though possessed by an uncommon force."

"A force," said the Assistant, "that normal intelligence cannot understand."

"Exactly. Neither normal nor uncommon intelligence: intelligence is not a tool capable of understanding my discourses. I speak to the people!"

"It's the ideal direction," murmured the First Assistant, softly.

The Cold

In the morning, they gave the Boss a map of the country, neatly folded, in color, so that the Boss would no longer confuse the North with the South, the Coast with the Interior, a large city with a small village, a castle with a modern shopping mall, a fountain with a tavern. In short, they gave the Boss a map of the country so that he would stop confusing everything with its opposite.

But since the Boss absentmindedly put the map in his pocket, by the afternoon he was already using it to blow his nose.

"This damn handkerchief they gave me!" he protested. "It'll break my nose!"

The two Assistants, who were very patriotic when there were witnesses—and in this case each was a witness for the other—were freezing, all along their spines, from head to toe: that just wasn't done. Neither gloves, nor an overcoat or a scarf could stop the shivers. Apart from which, it was a few degrees below zero.

"Oh, Boss. That is not a handkerchief: it's a map of the country!"

"Ah!" exclaimed the Boss, "that's why it's so rough!"

The Boss protested, shrugged his shoulders, and, since the damage had already been done, continued to blow his nose with the map.

"Blow your nose along the coast," suggested one of the Assistants. "It's the best way to avoid hurting your nose. It's softer."

The Boss suddenly stopped and fixed his gaze on his Assistant.

The atmosphere was somehow moving: such touching concern for his health. Without a word, the Boss leaned over and planted a small but significant kiss on his dedicated Assistant's head.

"I have already begun to read your chronicles, Mister Kraus. It's a pleasant world, isn't it?"

Mister Kraus smiled. Thanked him. Said his farewells.

The Boss Who Liked Movement

1

The Boss liked change because he did not like to stand still. And he did not like to stand still because he liked change. These were his views about the subject. The Boss had other views, but about other questions. About standing still and moving, these were his views. Two views.

He tried to alternate them. He was sometimes proud of one of them, and was sometimes proud of the other. The Boss would say, "This is called the commutative property of language. Just as two plus three is equal to three plus two, not liking being still is equal to liking movement. And furthermore: liking movement is equal to not liking being still. I don't know if you understood me?"

The two Assistants had understood.

"So," said the Boss, pointing to one of them, "you!"

"Me?!"

"Yes, you!"

"What did I do?"

"Nothing. That's the problem. We need to do things. We can't stand still. Have I already explained the question of the commutative property to you?"

"Yes, Boss. We really like it! It's five; three, plus two, it's five."

"By the looks of it you didn't understand. The results don't matter. What's important is the movement. Understood?"

The Boss's two Assistants understood. For the second time.

"Very well. Now, the two of you, while remaining seated, will stamp your feet on the floor, many times, until I order you to stop. Don't stop until the elections!"

"What a good idea, Boss."

2

While remaining seated, the two Assistants had been stamping their feet on the ground for several days now. The soles of their shoes had slowly disappeared and, inside their socks, whose material had practically evaporated, their feet burned, as though they were close to a fire. Both of them already had various wounds on their feet. However, the broad smile on the faces of the two Assistants had never flagged for an instant. "Movement was necessary, movement!" the Boss had said. Until the elections.

"Halt!" suddenly shouted the Boss, raising his arm. "I just remembered that we can do a movement that implies a change in space."

The two Assistants were amazed, their jaws dropped.

"With a change of space!"

"Space, how?"

"Oh, Boss, but couldn't . . ."

" . . . that be rather . . . hasty?"

"Our adversaries aren't expecting a sudden rupture," said the Boss. "Every once in a while we have to completely change our objectives and our plan of action."

"But it's four o'clock in the afternoon."

"It's time to get up."

"Excellent idea, Boss."

"Very well."

"This is what I thought. Tell me what you think of my solution. The two of you will swap chairs," continued the Boss. "Mister Assistant will go to Mister Assistant's chair. And Mister Assistant will go to Mister Assistant's chair."

"Boss, I didn't exactly understand how . . ."

"Neither did I," murmured the other.

"To explain it better. Mister Assistant on my right will go to the chair of Mister Assistant on my left. And Mister Assistant on my left will go to the chair of Mister Assistant on my right. At the same time."

"At the same time?"

"Yes, and vice versa."

"Vice versa?"

"Exactly. Then you stay in the new chair for an hour, an hour and a half . . ."

"Very well."

" . . . always stamping your feet on the ground . . ."

"Our feet . . ."

" . . . and then: vice versa again."

"What do you mean by vice versa again, Boss?"

"You change places again."

"There are only two chairs, Boss."

"Vice versa twice," asked the other Assistant, in a murmur, "isn't that the same as everything being exactly as it was before?"

"No, because it's a vice versa at the same time. In other words, you change places with your colleague, at the same time that your colleague changes places with you. Did you understand? It's a vice versa at the same time. A strategic concept."

Later, notwithstanding a couple of mix-ups, the two Assistants scrupulously followed instructions.

"Simultaneous vice versa and movement in space!" The Boss couldn't have been happier.

"Who's sleeping and who's running? Sometimes it isn't easy to tell them apart," said Mister Kraus.

To put on bedroom slippers or running shoes. These were the two choices. The most astute politicians were the ones who until the moment they actually put on their bedroom slippers seemed, after all, to be in the midst of intense athletic preparations.

"The origin of this optical illusion," murmured Mister Kraus, "can be called propaganda or myopia on the part of the observer."

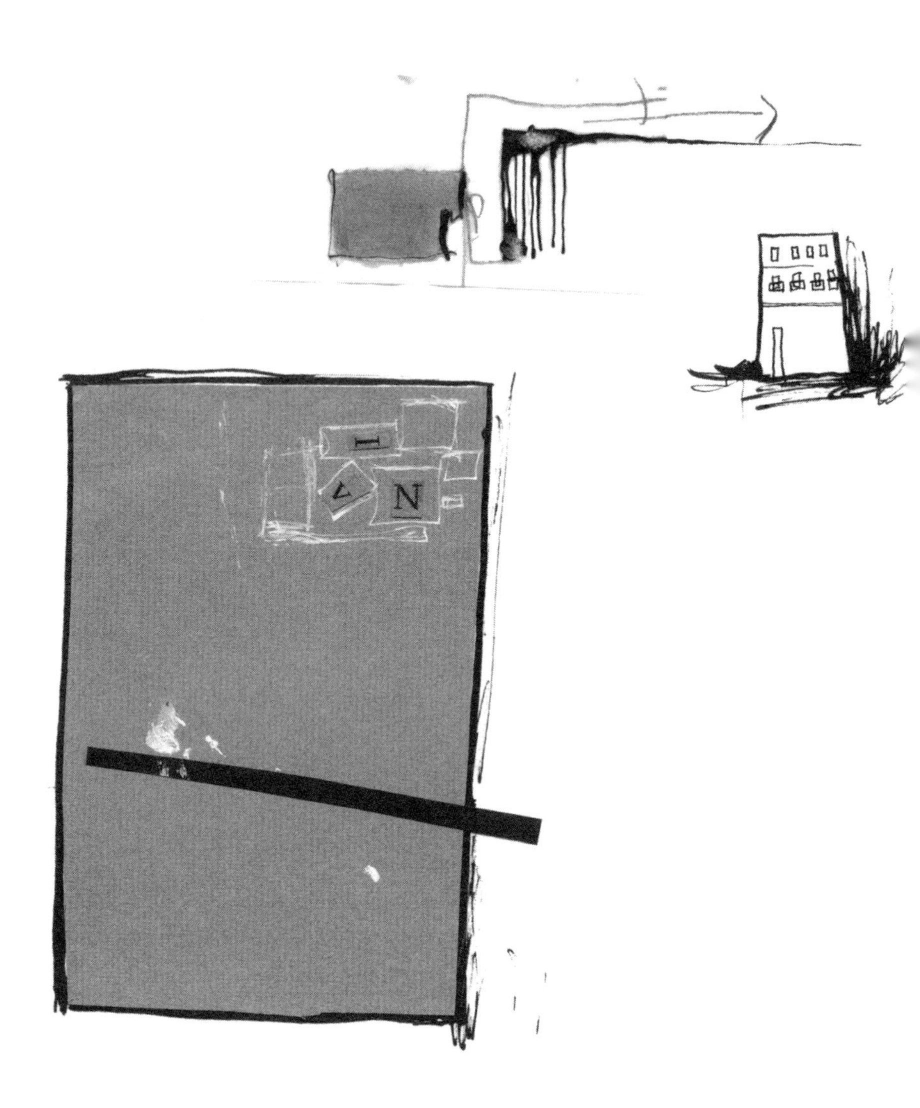
N

The Bridge

1

"This is the idea, Boss. We'll build two bridges, side by side. Each of them will have traffic in a single direction. On one bridge cars will go there, on the other bridge cars will come here. What do you think? Side by side, with less than fifty meters' distance between them. Close enough to wave from one bridge to the other. They will be like twin bridges. Two unprecedented bridges in Europe!"

And even in the world.

In the world!

The Boss shook his head and relied on a long silence. Then, in a grave voice, he said, "Before coming up with ingenious solutions, one must think about the money that will be spent. Because the money is not ours, it belongs to the people."

"Very well, Boss."

"Beautiful."

"Therefore, instead of two bridges, I propose that only one bridge be built, with traffic in both directions," said the Boss.

"Bravo! Excellent idea, Boss."

"Impressive."

"We'll cut expenditure by half," he added.

"By my sums, off the top of my head, exactly fifty percent," agreed the Assistant.

"Bravo, Boss!"

"Now, it's time to announce that we managed to reduce expenditure on this project by half. So that the people can see how zealous we are about public funds."

"Very well."

"I just think it's a pity," said the Boss, "that my excellent Assistants did not propose three bridges at the outset instead of two. If that had been the case, today we could have announced that expenditure had been reduced to one-third."

"You're right, Boss."

"We failed!" murmured the Assistant, lowering his eyes, ashamed.

2

The following day, however, the Boss had changed his mind.

"For reasons that are part of my inner intellectual core, which I don't think would be good manners to expose, I have decided that we are not going to build two bridges, nor one. We will build three bridges. Side by side. Or better: side by side by side. Each of them will have traffic in one direction only."

"How far apart from each other?"

"The exact distance hasn't yet been decided. I still have to do calculations. These decisions can't be made before a certain . . . but I'm aiming at fifty meters. I like the number."

The Assistant wrote it down in his notepad and underlined it: fifty meters!

"We will maintain the two bridges," continued the Boss, "each bridge will only have one-way traffic—one in this direction, the other in that direction—and the third bridge will be optional. In the morning, when a large number of cars are entering the capital, the third bridge will only have traffic from the suburbs toward the capital. And, at the end of the day, the direction will be capital–suburbs."

"Thus," exclaimed one of the Assistants, trying to contain his emotion, "thus we will always have two bridges open in the direction that is necessary to handle a greater flow of traffic!"

"Exactly," said the Boss.

"And we will be investing three times more in the modernization of our country than we would have invested with a single bridge!"

"Exactly!"

"And Boss . . ."

"Yes?"

"Boss!"

The Assistant's lips were trembling with emotion.

"Boss, Boss!"

"What is it, man!"

"Building three bridges side by side is even more unprecedented than building two."

"I hadn't even thought of that."

"It's extraordinary!"

·

About the politicians' penchant for putting forth numbers (or: about the importance of shoelaces), Mister Kraus said the following: "Any exact number flung at the eyes of an insecure and distracted population produces blindness.

"When they fling a number directly at our faces, we should pretend to be distracted, imitating certain comic actors from silent movies, and seize that exact moment to tie our shoelaces.

"When we finally straighten up again and raise our heads, the number will have already whizzed by, at a high speed, and will thus no longer affect our vision," continued Mister Kraus.

"If we wait a while, we will even be able to hear the number smashing against a wall into various uneven fragments.

"With our vision intact, we will then be able to witness the lamentable spectacle of the incoherent ruins of what, mere instants ago, had seemed to be an exact, convincing and decisive number."

Seated at the café, in his usual chair, Mister Kraus wrote some notes in his notebook.

About Political Speeches

One can't be sure of the size of people's feet from the size of their shoes.

There are two possibilities: either the feet are smaller than the shoes and the latter exaggerate the truth, or the feet are larger than the shoes and, thus sacrificed, the truth still remains hidden.

The Ineffectiveness of Vitamins

He thinks that vitamins will help infiltrate energy into his thoughts, but most therapeutic products are not creative; they do not invent anything: they merely reinforce preexisting qualities.

Punctuality

Some habits are never abandoned. A good politician will arrive late even for the inauguration of a clock.

T
S
O
M

Inaugurations

1

The Boss was nervous. He was walking from one side to the other.

"There is nothing to inaugurate, nothing! These men didn't even make a single chair. There is nothing to inaugurate!"

"Not even a needle, Boss."

"Not even a needle to inaugurate," murmured the other Assistant. "Not even a tiny needle!"

"Not even one like this," insisted the First Assistant, expressively putting his thumb and forefinger together. "Not even one like this! Like this!"

"Nothing!"

It was almost as though the two Assistants had been hypnotized by that monotonous discourse.

"Not even the eye of a needle has been done!"

"Nothing. Not even an eye of a needle."

"Not even half a needle."

"Not even half the eye of a needle."

"Nothing, nothing!"

"Enough!" yelled the Boss. "I can't stand listening to you any more!"

"We'll shut up, Boss."

"I have an idea," exclaimed the First Assistant, suddenly.

"Bravo!"

"This is my idea: Boss, have you ever been to this unpleasant, freezing, desolate, and from a certain point of view even disgusting place, which is nevertheless so promising?"

"Me? Of course not. Are you crazy?"

"Well, there it is!"

"What is there?!"

"We can inaugurate your presence in that place. It's the first time the Boss is going there. Isn't that extraordinary?"

"I'm beginning to like the idea. And it makes sense."

"Nothing so important will ever happen in that place!"

"Don't exaggerate," murmured the Boss, while he almost drowned with contentment in his own chin.

"Perhaps one of us should inaugurate your presence in that place, Boss. What do you think?"

"I myself will inaugurate my presence in that place!!"

"It isn't easy," said the two Assistants in unison.

"To inaugurate and to be inaugurated at the same time."

That was when, vigorously raising his chin toward the sky, the Boss responded, all at once, "I'm a man who likes to face difficulties head-on."

And, in fact, he was.

2

"Boss, everything that occupies volume has already been inaugurated in this blessed land where we have ended up!"

Once again they were disheartened. They looked around them: everything had already been inaugurated.

Some things had even been inaugurated centuries ago.

"This castle . . . ?"

"It's prior to Your Excellency's arrival."

"If everything that occupies volume in this place has already been inaugurated," said the Boss, "then we will have to think about things that don't occupy volume!"

"I hadn't thought of that, Boss."

"Actually I had thought of that," exclaimed the other Assistant, "but then I forgot."

"Very well," continued the Boss, ignoring the Assistants' vigorous murmurs, "here's an idea!"

"Where, Boss?!"

The Boss continued, "Here's my idea: has today ever occurred before in this place?"

"Boss, you want to know if at any time before today, today existed?"

"In this place, I'm only referring to this place," clarified the Boss.

"Never, Boss. It's the first time that this day has dawned in this place."

"There you have it!"

"What, Boss?"

"We can inaugurate this day in this place. I will inaugurate today."

"It's an impressive idea, Boss."

"Instead of inaugurating spaces, we can inaugurate time. Now that is undoubtedly an important idea."

The Boss paused. Silence reigned. He began again: "However, to only do one inauguration—that of today—doesn't seem very substantial. How long are we scheduled to stay in this place, dear Assistants?"

"According to the program, we're scheduled to stay here for two hours."

"Two hours? How many quarters of an hour does that give us?"

"Eight, Boss. Four quarters of an hour during the first hour, plus four during the second hour. Eight in all."

"Very well, we're not going to inaugurate today, but instead the quarters of an hour. Every fifteen minutes we will inaugurate the next fifteen minutes. Eight inaugurations."

The two Assistants were dumbfounded.

"So that was what you had in mind when you mentioned the possibility of inaugurating things which did not have volume, which did not occupy space."

"Essentially, to inaugurate things that are not visible," clarified the Boss.

"Exactly."

"Inaugurating the invisible! Oh, Boss, what an idea!!!"

3

"Essentially, the idea is to transmit this message: Everything that cannot be seen, we're the ones who did it."

"Excellent, that's exactly it."

"Because there are always contestations about what can be seen: I'm the one who did this, this was by him, et cetera, et cetera. You know how people are."

"People . . ."

"This way we can relax. Without being subject to criticism."

"Absolutely."

"We can say: look around you, look carefully around you: whatever you don't see, we're the ones who did it!!"

"Plus, we can even say: everything that cannot be seen didn't exist before us."

"That is excellent."

"Great slogan."

"If there are phrases that are capable of capturing the imagination of a crowd in a single stroke, this is one of them."

"Excellent, excellent!"

"But we should establish a limit," said one of the Assistants.

"A limit, how?"

"We should say something like: everything that is around us in an area of 150 square kilometers and cannot be seen, was made by us; before us it didn't exist."

"If we don't establish limits, we could point to things outside our country."

"And so?"

"So, people could get suspicious. How can we manage to do things—even if invisible—outside our country? For example, in a neighboring country?"

"You're right."

"Plus: if we say that whatever cannot be seen on the other side of the frontier was made by us, we risk being sued. It's a juridical question."

"You're right."

"We've done everything that can't be seen, but only within our borders. Is that it?"

"That's it."

"Seems fine to me."

"On that side, men following the Boss's orders fired shots toward the slower birds," said Mister Kraus.

On this side, the Boss picked up one or two injured birds and, in front of everyone, tried to heal them, dedicating himself passionately, day after day, exclusively to their recovery. Saving at least one of the birds had become an obsession.

A naïve man might think that it would have been easier not to have given orders to shoot at the birds in the first place. However, the process would be repeated the following year.

The Map

1

They had (once again) given the Boss a map of the country—it was already the fifth or sixth one. He had lost the earlier ones, or had written key words for his speeches on top of them, or had blown his nose in them, or had put them under a bottle of wine so as not to stain the table; in short: the Boss was absentminded.

However, he was also quite careful, in a certain way. For example: he would clean all the liquids and stains—wine and other substances—only with the part of the map that depicted the interior regions of the country—the most arid zone.

A more educated Assistant had tried, several months ago, to explain to the Boss that the map was merely a representation.

However, the Boss didn't understand. He paid no attention to technical pretentiousness. "I don't want to hear about theories," he would say.

In truth, the Boss had an intellectual problem: he could not distinguish reality from the representation of reality.

During a drought, after having decided to write "Rain!" with a pen on top of the region that needed water the most, he was absolutely baffled to find, later, that, in fact, it had not rained in that area.

Ceaselessly pondering which of his adversaries could be thwarting his energetic actions, the Boss murmured, intrigued, to himself, "But if I wrote 'rain' on the map . . ."

2

But as we have said, even so, the Boss was always losing or damaging maps of the nation. However, he was not completely distracted; for example: he always had with him, in the pocket on his right side, intact and well protected, the program guide for the various television channels.

There was a theory behind this: "Everything that doesn't fit inside the television," the Boss used to say, "does not belong to the country. It's outside our territory."

For him, the most authentic map of the country was the television set he had at home.

This was the Boss's personal vision.

"Why would I want a map?" he exclaimed. "What I need is to have every television channel on!"

"So," said one of the Assistants, "if I understood correctly, the Boss will see what happens on the different channels and will then act, with energetic measures or really very energetic measures, so as to resolve problems. Is that it?"

"More or less," answered the Boss. "It's necessary to expound slightly further."

There was silence in the hall. The Boss was gaining momentum.

"Expound, Boss."

"Expound, expound."

The Boss, in silence, concentrated, preparing himself to expound further.

3

The Boss expounded further. For this he used a particular technique, which was to repeat things.

"My concept of the border," repeated the Boss, "is defined by the lines that delimit the television screen. Everything that appears outside the screen does not belong to our country, it is already beyond the frontier. Do you understand?"

One of the Assistants took notes, while the other stared in amazement with his mouth wide open. They occasionally changed roles.

In the meanwhile, it was as though both of them were wracked by tremors. Tremors that were not corporal but an intellectual tremor. Both of them had the feeling that they were witnessing a unique moment, a moment in which an idea shot out to the world, for the first time, with the uncontrollable force of a bomb.

"Ah, if the Boss only had a bombardier," murmured one of the Assistants to himself. "Think of what he could do with even a single bombardier!"

After recovering his breath and allowing the Assistants time to practice their glances of uncontained admiration, the Boss said, in a decisive tone of voice, while, stretching his thumb out with the intensity of religious devotion, he pressed the switch on his screen, "This is my country."

4

The little Assistant, a figure who, despite his name, was a muscular giant who could always be found a few meters away from the Boss, on his guard, always prepared to quickly intervene in more intense intellectual discussions—the little Assistant insisted, "It would do no harm if the Boss studied a map of the country."

"I don't need to know geography!" the Boss had responded on that occasion, bothered. "What I need to do is prepare speeches. The most important thing is to know how to speak about the mountains. Who needs to know where the mountains are located?"

"But it's good to be familiar with the territory of the nation," insisted the giant. "So that not even a single square meter escapes from your orders."

There you had it. That final sentence had touched a chord with the Boss's most sensitive spot.

"Go on, go on."

"The advantage of being familiar with the country, especially its geography, is that you can thus send orders to every little corner. If you know your geography, your orders can be exhaustive, down to the last square meter. It's almost like having a sheet of paper with a grid of squares and filling up all the spaces with your directives. Without leaving even the tiniest elevation or a miserable stream outside the benevolent reach of your political measures."

"I hadn't thought of that."

"But think, do think," suggested the little Assistant. "Boss, do you think it's right that some little village, hidden behind a mountain of hay, should be deprived of the privilege of receiving at least one or two political orders per day from Your Excellency?"

"You're right," murmured the Boss. "Give me that map."

Opinion Polls

1

The elections were approaching and the opinion polls did not favor the Boss.

"The question is this," said the Boss, "when an individual, even one in full command of his brain, says that he is leaning to the left and not to the right, who can say that he is not thinking precisely the opposite?"

"That's a question one can always consider."

"Moreover," continued the Boss, "who is to say that when he says that he wants to go to the left he doesn't really want to go to the right?"

"I had already thought of that," murmured an Assistant.

"I had also thought of that," added the other.

"We both thought at the same time," the two agreed.

"Thus, my theory about opinion polls is, in the first place, the following, and let me explain . . ."

The two Assistants had already arranged their expressions in the form of an attentive ear.

The Boss continued, "It is not enough to obtain the opinion of the people. It is necessary to interpret it. Even when they only write a cross, what does that cross mean? Each personal opinion should be interpreted under a magnifying glass, by specialists."

"Who are. . . ?"

"Who are what I call: Specialists in Me."

"Therefore, specialists," murmured the Assistant, "in the study of the human mind, human personality. . . ?"

"Who said anything about humans?!" retorted the Boss, later emphasizing the first word. "I said, specialists in Me. In Me, get it?!"

"Ah, experts specializing in Your Excellency, in the Boss."

"Well, there you are! Finally! And who is the best specialist in Me, I ask? Who is best qualified to interpret the subjective opinion of the highly subjective individuals of this nation? Who is the best specialist in Me?"

"Your Excellency?" hazarded the Assistants.

"Exactly. Me! Me! I am the one who will objectively interpret the subjective opinion of the people."

"Bravo! That's science."

2

"Very well," accepted the Boss, finally. "If the opinion polls want to resort to the participation of the people, so be it."

"They are talking about random samples."

"Random? How imprudent!"

"Random, but not that random. Despite everything, there is an order to it. With a certain number of women, men, et cetera. It's all very scientific."

"Let them keep the scientific element of opinion polls, I always liked science. But the units of this science should be defined by me."

"How, Your Excellency, Boss?"

"The proposal that seems to me to be the fairest and most balanced solution of all is as follows: the opinion poll should be extended to a sample that is as large as possible: men, women, youths, senior citizens. And others as well."

"Even the others?"

"Even the others."

"This is democracy!"

"Long live democracy!" yelled the other Assistant immediately.

"And they should all be given my phone number."

"What?"

"My phone number," said the Boss. "Each one of the elements of this representative sample, chosen randomly according to scientific criteria, should call me to find out my opinion. Thus we will have a fair opinion poll, with an extended sample, and an objective and pondered opinion."

"Thus, Boss, you suggest that instead of giving their opinion, the opinion poll sample call you for you to give your opinion to everyone."

"One at a time."

"And they won't be able to accuse us of tampering with the results?"

"Of course not. The question will always be asked by a different person. This is what we have to highlight. Any member of the population can ask my opinion. How can one manipulate the data if the people themselves are the ones asking me questions?"

"You're right, Boss."

"And it's original."

"What is important in a television debate?"

Mister Kraus responded, "Argumentative profoundness loses (by a K.O.) in the face of the quality of eyebrow movement. How many votes is a certain twitch of the nose at an incisive moment worth?! The answer would shake the foundations of our faith in democracy," murmured Mister Kraus.

Dialogue (One Day before the Elections)

"This thing about a balanced view, holding ballots at all times and just about everywhere."

"We are living in a century of democracy: the people should have a say in everything."

"Even those whose voice . . ."

"Even those people."

"Therefore: the people would decide everything."

"I was talking, for example, about a game of football."

"A game that is nothing more than a dictatorship by the players."

"So what you are proposing is . . ."

"I'll repeat that: the decision should be left to the spectators of a match and not the players."

"Very well."

"Instead of twenty-two players and a referee deciding the outcome of the game, the thirty thousand spectators would do so. By voting. It's a vast difference. You only need to do the math."

"Only the spectators present in the stadium would be able to vote?"

"Yes."

"That's fair."

"And an excellent way of inducing people to go and watch the match. They would actually be responsible for deciding the outcome. It would be worth making the trip. I don't think it's fair to leave something so important—like the outcome of a match—only in the hands (or feet) of fewer than two dozen citizens."

"In this case, called: football players."

"Exactly."

"The outcome of the matches would then be decided not by momentary skills but by pondered decisions by the population."

"It seems fair to me. We are living in a century of intelligence and votes."

"A football match decided by a popular vote (especially by the spectators) and not on account of goals by players! It's changes like this that transform a backward country into a developed nation."

"Yes."

"Instead of decisions wrought by a knee, instead of decisions like that, muscular, physical, noncerebral, and undemocratic decisions, they would now be broad-based decisions."

"Each football match would thus be a kind of referendum."

"Yes, but please do note that first the game would have to be played."

"The matches would be missed."

"The decisions would be made after the match—and serious individuals would determine which team emerged victorious, irrespective of the goals that were scored, without being influenced by the emotions that could have existed before, after reflecting logically about what really happened."

"Having passionate matches is not worthy of a century where rationality requires that events be handled differently."

"Exactly."

"Rationality and democracy, the importance of each citizen's opinion and vote: that's where the future of football lies."

"It's only fair."

"What about the elections to determine who governs the nation?"

"Ah, in this regard, I think we should hold an old-fashioned football match: each Party would choose eleven players and the team that scored the most goals would govern."

"That seems sensible and rational."

"Worthy of this century."

"Yes. Worthy of this century."

The elections were over and the sweeper had been pushing the ballot slips toward the corner of the hall with his broom for over two hours.

The now useless ballot slips advanced against their will toward the corner as though they were dirty napkins and not papers that had been decisive for a certain nation at a certain time. They were pushed about like trash. Mister Kraus observed the entire spectacle melancholically.

The day after the elections, in the café, at his habitual table, Mister Kraus noted in his notebook:

A posteriori observation 1

In their contacts with the simpler elements of the population, some politicians kiss people on the cheek almost like someone on a wharf bidding farewell to a boat setting sail never to return.

The relationship between politicians and the people

After an animated electoral campaign, the great advantage of any democratic election is that the people finally leave the politicians' drawing rooms.

It's a feeling of relief that some elected representatives describe as being similar to the moment in which an intense pain, for some obscure reason, comes to an end.

A posteriori observation 2

When politicians kiss senior citizens, they remind one of the first timid bite of a worm on a body that no longer has the means to flee nor a door from which to exit.

After the Elections

After any election, politicians—irrespective of whether they have won or lost—always have the feeling that the more profound people have all just boarded a train, heading, compactly, for a distant land. This population will come back, on the same train, only in the weeks preceding the next election.

This interval is essential so that the politicians have time to delicately transform hate or indifference into a new genuine passion.

"The words of the winner always seem to be more intelligent," murmured someone.

"It remains to be seen whether this is due to the quality of the words themselves or the noise that the crowd makes when it gets together, which prevents one from hearing," responded Mister Kraus.

But the chronicles continued even after the elections.

The Day after the Elections

1

"Well, did you win?!"

"Yes, I won."

"So, you are therefore the Boss."

"From this moment onward, exactly: the Boss. And you, what do you do?"

"I eliminate redundancies."

"Very well."

"For example, if there were two Bosses I would eliminate one. It's part of my job description. I even have a dagger."

"Just as well the result wasn't a tie."

"That was lucky! But look, sometimes even when there is only one Boss . . ."

"And do you work alone?"

"Nobody likes to work alone. In truth, I work with another official who tries to ensure that everything is always explained clearly."

"Wonderful."

"These joint efforts result in a balance between a little and a lot. Too many explanations and too few explanations. I don't know if you are following my drift?"

"I am, and it seems to be sensible."

"Our work method is as follows: my colleague advances first and explains too much, then I appear and I say: it was unnecessary for my colleague to have explained this, this, and this. That and that and that were excessive."

"Very well. It's a strategy."

2

"I apologize for asking again, but Boss, what is your name?"

"Just call me Boss."

"With a B?"

"Yes."

"That's the same name as the last Boss."

"We are all from the same country. Hence the coincidence."

"Hence the B."

"Exactly."

"In my opinion, it's very wise. It prevents mistakes with names."

"That's one of the advantages."

"However, there is the question of the small b or the big B. We have one Boss with a big B, as of yesterday: Your Excellency. Bosses with a small b, we have one for every ten square meters."

"Is that a lot?"

"This pavilion alone has three hundred square meters, so Boss, with a big B, you can do the math and see how many bosses we have with a small b."

"If we have a boss with a small b for every ten square meters, in three hundred square meters we have . . ."

"We have. . . ?"

"Thirty bosses with a small b!"

"Exactly, thirty. Isn't that a crazy number?"

"No: three hundred divided by ten: thirty. What craziness are you talking about?"

"I was talking of the underlying concept. Look, even I, who obey almost everybody, am the boss, with a small b, of two or three wretches. Only the last one on the list is not a boss."

"It seems unfair."

"So, we have a new Boss?!"

It was Mister Henri, already in a conversational state par excellence.

Without slowing his pace, Mister Kraus merely responded, "At first glance, at first glance!"

X

The Return

1

The Assistants were radiant: it had already been weeks since they had assisted anyone, but now all that desire to Assist could once again be applied.

Many of them had tried during the period when the Boss had been absent, but it was as though the objects of their assistance seemed to flee from them. Some, the astute ones, did actually flee. It was quite visible: they ran; they placed one foot after the other and disappeared from sight: it was a fact, those who needed their services fled when the Assistants approached them. Elderly individuals, who had difficulties understanding and moving, even they, with a sudden and surprising burst of vitality, fled. They escaped, they dived into narrow dark alleys—little old men and little old ladies, that's who we are talking about—and, suddenly, they disappeared, nobody saw them again. And the Assistants had no work to do. They only wanted to assist.

Now this entire period had come to an end. The Boss was back!

Many of the Assistants were so happy that they even underwent profound physiological changes. Their hearts beat like only the hearts of wild men beat. In silence, one of the Assistants, feeling his heart beat to the rhythm of ancient manhunts, had even murmured to himself, "I don't even seem to be a civilized man!" He was moved.

The Boss was back; the Boss, the Boss, the Boss was back!

2

"Things could have progressed in my absence, but the question is: What is progress? And why are there such preconceived notions about going back, about delaying, about hesitating?"

"Exactly, Boss."

Little was known about the city, but that, yes, it was a fact: the Assistants' hearts now beat better! With more intelligence, one could almost say, had the heart not been an organ that specialized in other matters.

But there was work to be done.

"Boss, we have here a series of reports that have been held up and a series of real things that are progressing! Boss, you have to deal with this!"

"I have never seen anything like this," added the other Assistant.

"When I left, things were proceeding in another direction," said the Boss.

"Not just in another direction . . . ," added the first Assistant.

"They were proceeding in precisely the opposite direction!"

"Exactly," agreed the second Assistant, "real things were held up and it was the reports that were moving."

"Very well," said the Boss, "there is no time to lose. We now have to proceed at great speed in the direction of the past."

"That's it, Boss."

3

The Boss was back.

"There is, for example," said an Assistant, "the question of the public works and the question of the demolitions."

The Boss paused (how they had missed these pauses) and began, "I have reflected about this matter and come to the following conclusion: the essential thing is to not do the two things at the same time and in the same space."

"How, Boss?"

"It seems to me," said the Boss, "that the best thing is to knock down in one space and build up in another space. So as not to confuse things. In fact, I would like to say that the new concept that I will develop during my return is the concept of . . ."

"Of?"

"Of . . ." (the Boss was wont to raise his eyebrows a lot, like someone who has just formulated a riddle). "It's the concept of building upward but downward! Isn't it an exemplary idea? We knock down old buildings and we build new structures on top that will tumble down; and this because, in a certain way, things later always end up by falling down."

"It's almost a philosophical concept."

"Yes, without doubt," said the Boss who while resuming his office seemed to have the enthusiasm of a youngster, "it's a concept that introduces the perception of time. Everything changes, my dear assistants, and everything that is erected, later falls. Thus, from today onward, we are going to be the first city that constructs with the lucidity of perceiving that everything is temporary—*temporarium tudio*—therefore: we will knock buildings down and we will build buildings on top to fall down."

"Bravo, Boss. With so much philosophy we can even save on cement."

"I hadn't thought of that."

The Parking Lot

Keeping in mind the existence of innumerable individuals from among the people, the clergy, and even the nobility, who do not understand anything about engines or automobiles, the Boss said, "Enough!"

And after gaining momentum, uttered the following declaration:

"Enough!"

"Which means. . .?" someone asked.

"It means that it's enough," clarified the Boss.

"Enough, you mean?"

"Exactly."

The old democratic tradition of giving cars of different qualities, according to the hierarchical position of the receiver, just did not seem adequate to him.

He thought it was important that, at first glance, even an absolute ignoramus who knew nothing about brands, the pickup, and the engine should be able to distinguish a mere director-general from a minister.

It was for this excellent reason that he recommenced lauding the nonpolluting benefits of bicycles traversing the city.

Bicycles: do you know of any technology that is more modern than bicycles?

Thus, in the parking lot reserved for elements of the government, there was now space for: one automobile, two motorcycles, four bicycles, nine horses; and there was even space for more than twenty donkeys.

As the prevailing norms about respect for the hierarchy affirm, and despite the difference in speeds attained on straight stretches, those who came on donkeys habitually arrived first.

"It's child's play," said Mister Kraus. "When politicians speak to us from the heavens above, and point their fingers upward saying, See?, it's then, at that precise moment, that we should be looking attentively at the objects they have in their cellars."

About an Enlightened Government

There were so many ministers that during general meetings it was necessary to hire one of those ushers from the cinema theater whose job was to take viewers to their designated seat.

Since, by an age-old tradition, cabinet meetings—just like films—were held in the dark, the usher with his flashlight was (literally) the only one who could see something before him.

As each minister arrived, the usher took him, always guided by his little flashlight, through the various rows, until they reached his place in the cabinet.

"This row, third chair from the far side."

Apologizing to the other ministers, the new arrival made his way to his seat, stepping on people's feet more or less frequently.

As soon as the man with the flashlight left, the hall became pitch dark, without a speck of light to be seen; and it had thus become a normal practice for the Boss to immediately say, calming his colleagues with his voice, "I am here, I am here!"

After they had located the Boss, by the sound of his voice, the meeting would begin.

Seated in his habitual chair, hunched over, Mister Kraus prepared his next chronicles and scribbled some notes in his notebook.

"Causes" of an enigmatic constitution

He complained that he did not even have time to eat, he was so dedicated to the public cause. However, he increasingly put on weight. Thus, everybody around him was convinced that the public cause had a lot in common with an excess of calories.

Reasons for resigning

Any nation must be managed sensibly and by means of a careful and considered use of intelligence. Thus, whenever a politician falls in love, he should immediately give up his seat.

Verbal punctuality

A certain politician repeated the same words so many times at the same monotonous rhythm that his colleagues used to set the hour hand on their watches according to the word "freedom" and the minute hand according to the word "democracy."

Legal, and Other, Decisions

1

"Since I am a human being, any approved law that harms even a single individual is a law that persecutes me as an individual. At least that's how I see it."

These were words of solidarity from the Boss, who was very attached to the population—all the more since there was now a pressing need to put an end to the constant protests that had begun to appear after any changes were made in the law.

It was just that, in fact, there was always a group of people who felt harmed.

The legislators then tried to create a law that did not harm anyone, not even a single person; but they were unable to do so.

Even when they made laws about the trees or the wind, it never worked. There were always protests. And human protests.

But the Boss insisted, "Make a law that does not harm anyone, not a single person, not a senior citizen, nor a wretch. That's all I ask."

"What you are asking for is not a law, Boss, it's a miracle," said the Assistants.

"And who deals with this kind of special law?" immediately asked the Boss.

Suddenly, the hall fell silent.

The Assistants were embarrassed. Nobody knew how to give the Boss a definite answer.

At the back of the hall, in the midst of the general silence and immobility, one of the new Assistants dared to raise his hand.

"Tell me, Mister Assistant, there at the back."

"Boss, I don't know the entire organogram, but if there is no governmental department responsible for miracles, I suggest that one be created."

"An excellent idea," said the Boss, enthused.

However, from the expression on his face, one could immediately see that this solution raised new and profound questions: Would there be enough space on the sheet of paper used for the organogram to accommodate yet another department?

2

The legislator arrived almost leaping with enthusiasm: he had found a formula for a decree that seemed to fulfill the objective: to make a law that did not harm anyone.

"And what is this formula, my dear legislator?"

"It's simple. Here it is." And he read, "This law decides that this law does not decide anything."

"But is that a law?"

"If this sentence—because, essentially, Excellency, laws are sentences—if this sentence were published as a legal decree it would become a decree-law."

"This law decides that this law does not decide anything," murmured the Boss to himself, like someone repeating a verse that fascinates him.

"It's a thoroughly modern law, don't you think?"

"Yes, while seeming to be a conformist law, it is a drastic law after all."

"Because people . . . ," the Boss began to say, but then fell silent.

"Yes, more precisely: what everybody would like is for nothing to change, but for life to improve."

"Ah, it's not going to be easy."

"No. But if we continue with this line of laws, there is a series of variations that could be developed. For example, 'This law decides that things can be done in one way or any other way.' How about that? Isn't this also a law that fits perfectly into the objective of making laws that do not incite any kind of protest? 'This law decides that things can be done in one way or any other way.' It's a brilliant formula, even if I say so myself. Yes, it's not bad. But I always liked making concrete, objective laws, which people can understand."

"Oh, Boss, don't be stubborn."

3

The Boss was not convinced. He liked the sound of the law, its rhythm, the way it began and ended, however the contents of the law, they didn't quite convince him.

It was as though something was missing. That was it: something was missing here. But what?

The Boss repeated the sentence again, this time out loud: "'This law decides that things can be done in one way or any other way.' I know!" murmured the Boss. "I know what I think is missing. It's a very individual perception, I acknowledge that, but here it is: this law is about allowing one to do something in one way or in any other way—very well, but the question is: What? What is this law talking about?"

"That is never stated explicitly," murmured, condescendingly, the older Assistant, "it's always ambiguous, undetermined. Mention is made of something as though everybody knows what that something is. I don't know what that something is, you don't know, nobody knows; however, you can be sure of one thing: the people like this kind of law."

"They do?"

"Of course they do. To be able to do something in one way or in any other way? Is there anyone who would not like this kind of imposition?"

"But what will this change?" asked the Boss. "What will change, for example, with, 'This law decides that this law does not decide anything'?"

"Nothing changes."

"Nothing?"

"Nothing. But that is what the people want."

"What I want, you know," exclaimed the Boss, in his enthusiastic tone of voice, "what I want is to do everything, I mean everything, for the people!"

"Then, Boss, don't do anything; they won't notice the difference."

"Profound reading," murmured Mister Kraus. "Politicians don't read books; at most they read the titles. They do the same thing with people."

About the Nation's Aircraft

1

"Dear Assistants, I am very angry."

"Why, Boss? Some other unpleasant news?"

"No, today it isn't because of the newspapers, it's because of the world."

"Ah, so it isn't such a serious matter!"

"That's not the question: they told me that we do not have even half an aircraft to fight fires. Is that true?"

"It isn't true," said one Assistant, indignantly, "it isn't true!"

"It isn't true," said the other Assistant.

"We have half an aircraft," affirmed the First Assistant.

"We have half an aircraft!" emphasized the second.

"We have two half-aircraft," added the First Assistant, raising two of his little fingers high into the sky.

"Two?"

"Yes, two half-aircraft."

"And how much does that make?" asked the Boss.

"Two half-aircraft make one completely whole aircraft."

"One?" exclaimed the Boss, raising a finger to indicate his indignation.

"Yes, two halves: one. Half plus half."

"But apart from that helicopter that works," said the First Assistant, "we also have another helicopter that does not work."

"That also counts," murmured the Second Assistant.

"And what does it do?" asked the Boss.

"It observes."

"Vigilance."

"It's very alert."

"The helicopter?"

"And the radio works!"

2

"It's more a question of a concept."

"A concept, how?" asked the Boss.

"When they say that we do not have aircraft to fight fires one feels like saying: What do you know about the concept of aircraft?"

"Exactly, that's what one feels like saying," agreed the other Assistant.

"It's that there are two kinds of aircraft," explained the First Assistant. "High aircraft and low aircraft. The high aircraft . . ."

" . . . are those that fly," completed the Second Assistant.

"Low aircraft . . ."

" . . . are those that don't fly!" completed the Boss, with a smile of satisfaction (he loved to complete sentences).

"Exactly!"

"While it's true that we do not have many aircraft that fly, we have a vast quantity of aircraft that run."

"A vast quantity," added the Second Assistant.

"But these low aircraft," murmured the Boss, "trained to fight fires are . . . cars?"

"No, Boss."

"They're the firemen!!"

"The firemen?"

"Exactly, the firemen. But forget that word. The new name for fireman, adopted by us, is precisely that of LOW AIRCRAFT."

"And the firemen's fire trucks?"

"Not all of them are out of order."

3

"Therefore, high aircraft are those that fly, low aircraft are those that do not fly."

"Exactly."

"But we then had to subdivide them into two more categories; among the low aircraft there are high low aircraft and low low aircraft."

"How?"

"We established a reference: one meter and seventy-five centimeters. Firemen who are shorter than one meter and seventy-five centimeters are classified as low low aircraft. They never attack a fire from above."

"Very well."

"Firemen who are taller than one meter and seventy-five centimeters are then classified as high among the category of low aircraft."

"Very well."

"Keeping in mind our human resources, and this management of heights, we further decided that only firemen who are less than one meter and seventy-five centimeters would go inside the helicopter. Thus, on the ground we have more apparently low, but high, aircraft."

"A good strategic decision."

"Yes."

"There is just one problem," murmured the Boss, suddenly.

Everybody was quiet. The Boss was pondering the matter and he had raised one arm.

"The problem," said the Boss, "is that, by considering the firemen to be low aircraft it is true that we will have an abundance of aerial resources."

"Yes?"

"But we will then no longer have any terrestrial resources!"

"Oh, Boss, we didn't think of that!"

Some neighbors fortuitously ran into Mister Kraus and commented, "I have been reading your chronicles in the newspaper . . ."

But before they could continue, Mister Kraus smiled, expressed his appreciation for the compliment with a slight movement of his head, murmured half a handful of polite words, and continued on his way, "I'm late! Sorry."

"At least a pistol," said Mister Kraus that day, when he had moved away, on the verge of yelling. "It's reasonable not to use a sword during the twenty-first century! But at least a pistol."

An Exemplary Boss

The Boss liked to give examples. But apart from this he did not like to give anything to anyone.

When some wretch approached him, saying, "I need some funds to invest in my company," the Boss would immediately respond with the sentence, "Look, for example," and would then embark on a long speech where he did, in fact, exemplify.

When the wretch returned home, his wife asked him, "So, the Boss? Did he support you?"

And the man responded, "He gave me an example."

On other occasions, they had very concrete requests for the Boss.

For example, that he should order a pothole in a road to be repaired—because the hole had already caused various accidents.

"Oh, Boss, would it be possible to order that pothole to be repaired?! It's dangerous! And it won't cost much to have it fixed. It will take only two hours to repair it."

Even so, the Boss did not desist. "It's not quite that simple, you see . . . ," he would begin, and soon went on to say, "look, for example . . ."

And he would give his example.

Conversations when people returned home after talking to the Boss were therefore fairly repetitive:

"So, did the Boss give orders to proceed with repairs on the road?"

"No. He gave me an example."

Paying More Taxes Is Very Good for Those Who Pay More Taxes

1

"Essentially, it is . . ."

"Exactly, Boss. Essentially!"

The Boss coughed, he was in the middle of a sentence—it was not yet a suitable moment for servile interruptions.

"Essentially, it is," the Boss began again, irritated, "a problem of belief, not money."

"Of belief, Boss?" murmured the First Assistant.

"Yes, of belief. We have to transmit the idea that taxes are good for the people who pay taxes. The more they pay, the better it is for them. That is what they have to believe."

"Oh, Boss . . ."

"And we have to transmit this in a pedagogical manner; also using, as far as possible, complex formulae and complex economic theories."

"But isn't that what we're constantly doing?" murmured the First Assistant.

"Aren't we being sufficiently complex?" asked the second, fearfully.

"That's precisely it!" said the Boss, all at once. "Sometimes you simplify things, and that is fatal."

"Life is never simple," immediately philosophized one of the Assistants.

"Exactly. We must therefore invest even more in technical and obscure publicity. We must invest more in complexity."

"We have to hire more economists!"

"That's it."

2

"It's simple: taxes serve to improve the nation's living standards. Right?"

"Right."

"Therefore . . ."

"Therefore: the more taxes an individual pays, the more the nation's living standards improve."

"In other words . . ."

"In other words: the less money that each person has per month on which to live—owing to the fact of paying more taxes—the more money the nation has in general. At most: when somebody buys some bread and butter and eats it, he is, objectively, stealing the bread and butter from the nation."

"In other words: the worse each individual citizen lives the better for the nation."

"Exactly."

"So, long live the nation!" exclaimed the First Assistant.

The second assistant agreed.

"The question is: Are we here to serve the interests of individual citizens or the nation as a whole?"

"The nation as a whole, Boss!" yelled the Assistants in unison.

And they repeated it again, with their arms raised, "As a whole! As a whole!"

"And the nation belongs to everyone!" insisted the First Assistant.

"Exactly. To everyone!"

"Therefore, if our patriotic objective is to improve the nation's living standards, what we have to do is . . ."

"Worsen the living standards of each citizen!"

"That's it!"

"Some politicians interpret the word 'people' as though it were one of their pseudonyms," said Mister Kraus. He then murmured, "Democracy!" And fell silent.

He then further added, "In optimistic statistical terms, if the common man decided four times on the basis of his intelligence and another four times leaving it to chance, he would have four chances of getting it right."

His neighbor, Mister Henri, nodded his agreement.

The List of Contents

1

An enormous committee of Economists entered the central halls. They had brought a gigantic report. It was a prognosis; it contained the state of the nation's economy, in great detail. Three months of work involving more than thirty-two thousand Economists. They were well paid, it's true, but they deserved it: the report had over six hundred pages. And a list of contents.

The Boss opened up the report at the list of contents.

"This is a great help. It makes consulting the report so much easier," said the Boss, surprised.

"It helps a lot," agreed the President of the Committee of Economists. "You can see the subject in question here and later, a few spaces ahead, there is the page number."

"What an excellent idea!!" exclaimed the Boss.

"It has already been used in other works by other people; even outside politics. And even in other countries. When the reports are very large, there are even more detailed indications of the page numbers, so that readers do not waste a lot of time finding the subject that is of interest to them."

The Boss was fascinated. That question of the contents. What an idea!! He was undoubtedly surrounded by the best people. These Economists!!

"Impressive, this list of contents," insisted the Boss.

And he ran his forefinger all over this initial page of the report, from left to right, from top to bottom, with the meticulous gestures of a blind person feeling adapted writing.

"Here it is!" murmured the Boss, still enthusiastic. "For example, if I were interested in the item 'widespread poverty,' I go to the contents and here it is: page 322. It's extraordinary! Widespread poverty: page 322. How wonderful!"

"It's the list of contents, Boss."

2

The Boss continued to be fascinated with the list of contents of the report about the economy.

"Extraordinary!"

"It's useful, no doubt, but it's only a list of contents," murmured someone from the back, already irritated.

"The important thing is that the Boss likes something," whispered one of the Assistants to the President of the Economists, who was becoming rather disheartened. They had written about all the nation's problems. With thousands of calculations, numbers and numbers, practical and theoretical solutions. And the Boss: nothing. He was fascinated by the list of contents, euphoric: like the first Man to have heard a telephone working.

The President of the Committee of Economists, getting increasingly impatient, tried to control himself. "It's just a question of organization. It's a list of contents, nothing. But farther ahead we have presented four fundamental proposals to resolve the problem of poverty in the nation."

While speaking, he attempted with his hands, albeit always delicately, to force the Boss to go to the middle of the report.

However, responding with unflinching vigor, the Boss would not let him. The Report continued to remain open at the page with the list of contents. Until the end of the session.

"It's very important," insisted the Boss, keeping his two hands, solidly and firmly, on the page with the list of contents, seemingly not having heard anything at all. "This is an example of organization that should be applied to the entire nation. Everything: from top to bottom. From left to right. The entire nation should have a list of contents."

"We have four proposals," someone still ventured to say, but the voice soon faded away.

"It's just the list of contents," murmured the President of the Committee, who had already thrown in the towel: his arms hung low.

"Boss," asked one of the Assistants at the end, "should I send the Report to Education?"

Mister Kraus had handed over his last chronicle to the newspaper. The end of the day neared, like yesterday, and shortly a new Boss would appear in the world, then another and another. However, it was always the same.

The Fall

It was one of those cold days and breathing became a public act.

"Nobody breathes discreetly on these very cold days," said the Boss.

And it was true: when one exhaled, it cut a trail through the air, as though the air were painted or etched out with another color. On such days breathing was no longer a private act or something shared only by passionate couples. Breathing was like a speech, except at a much lower volume.

"Exhaling becomes almost as visible as singing."

"It's true."

"Like a voice that doesn't speak," said the Boss.

"Your breathing does, in fact, look magnificent!" said the Assistant, suddenly, as though he had just remembered something.

The Assistant continued, "Your Excellency, on cold days like this, you do not even need to say anything. Just by looking at the air that emanates from inside Your Excellency it is clear that in case Your Excellency did decide to speak, you would speak as never before. Your air is magnificent!" he repeated.

The Boss thanked him, trying to present a modest expression. He was good at that; like an acrobat: the Boss knew how to make faces. He kept them tucked away somewhere like one keeps small slips of paper in one's pockets with telephone numbers. When one needs a number one only has to find the right piece of paper in one's pockets. It was the same thing with him: he looked for an appropriate expression for the moment inside himself. And he took only about a thousandth of a second to find the thing. He was trained.

"You exaggerate," he told the Assistant.

"No, no, it's magnificent. Nobody exhales like that!"

In truth, the Boss heard these words like someone who hears that two plus two equals four. Someone was stating the obvious: he was excellent from all points of view, and his breathing—especially his exhalation—was magnificent! He felt in a certain way that the world, not from a general point of view, but the concrete world, nature, the elements of the atmosphere, should, together, if they could talk and were well-bred, thank him for that brilliant way of expelling carbon dioxide. "Nobody expels carbon dioxide like I do," thought the Boss. However, externally, he resumed his exclamations of modesty, "You exaggerate, Assistant. My exhalation is simply air."

"Air?!" exclaimed the Assistant. "No, not at all. It's something else. There's something about the way in which your exhalation stands out from the rest of the atmosphere that is reminiscent of ancient mythological stories. There is something secret and mysterious about it."

The Boss was enjoying listening to his Assistant, that music lulled him pleasantly, so to speak. In fact, they had climbed the stairs up to the fourth floor and he had barely noticed it.

Then, at that precise moment, he discovered a law that blended the world of physiology and psychology: being praised made one forget fatigue. "If someone," thought the Boss to himself, "was lauded every step of the way, he could easily climb to the top of the Eiffel Tower on foot." He was so enamored of this idea that he even stopped to write it down in a notebook. When he had time, he would sell that line of reasoning to athletes who needed it.

Epilogue

The Boss and his two Assistants were already on the balcony of the fourth floor, standing and braving the cold. One of the Assistants was out of his mind with jubilation, he was almost hopping.

"See, Boss, your exhalation. It's extraordinary, do you see this color?!" The Assistant pointed his forefinger at the plume of carbon dioxide that emanated from the Boss's mouth. "It's magnificent, magnificent!"

The Boss smiled, but it seemed to him that his Assistant was beginning to exaggerate: what the hell, he was the Boss, but his lungs and all the channels responsible for expelling the air from inside him were just the same as any other human being's. "I'm a man just like everyone else," he thought. However, he trusted his Assistant. If he said that his exhalation was particularly magnificent, then it was because it was true. The Boss then bent over to better observe the air coming out of his mouth.

"Yes, it's uncommon, but . . ."

"See it more closely," said the Assistant. "Bend over; you'll see it better if you're closer."

The Boss contained his joy—"Really, what a thing, even my air stands out, what an extraordinary thing!"—and with his belly pressed against the upper part of the balustrade on the balcony, he continued to bend forward. He wanted to see what emanated from his most profound depths from close up.

"That's it," continued the Assistant, "when your exhalation

comes down from above, something comes out there . . . an unusual authority!"

They were, as has been mentioned above, on the fourth floor. And it was then that it happened.

As he was in the middle of a compliment, the Assistant didn't make it in time to prevent the tragedy. The Boss really wanted to see what the air he exhaled looked like when it blew out vertically, from top to bottom. So he bent farther forward. And even farther. And farther. And farther. And farther.

Until he didn't have enough time to turn back.

Mister Walser

1

Mister Walser was overjoyed! In the midst of bushes, wild plants, and other manifestations of nature, in the course of a full and unpredictable life, this was what he had managed to build—using all the specialized technical skills that only a great civilization is capable of providing—a simple house, nothing luxurious or ostentatious, a modest home in which to live, the house of Mister Walser, a man who, for the time being, was alone in the world, but someone who viewed this house that had finally been finished—how many years had it taken to build?! so many!—as an opportunity to, frankly speaking, find company at last.

If until then the absence of a closed, comfortable space, exclusively his, had been an insurmountable hurdle, now, surrounded by that all-pervading smell of newness that emanated from the wood, the paint on the walls, even the sound of the machines that were necessary for his domestic life as a single man living on his own, well, now, with the new house, everything seemed possible. For Mister Walser, his house was not merely a place that humanity had conquered from the surrounding forest, from the space that nonhuman things seemed to have claimed as their own—it was also an ideal landscape to begin to talk with other men—and he really felt the need to do just that.

Walser promised himself that he would always have the day's newspaper. He was well aware that the geographical isolation of his house meant, essentially, maintaining the physical presence, and in a certain way also the spiritual presence, of human events alive. And this was an indispensable task, all the more so because Walser had refused from the very outset any possibility of installing any technical device that allowed access to images. Only the newspaper. Nothing more than that.

2

It is said that this expectation of creating a personal space where it was possible to simply talk with other men, argue, discuss large or small ideas, matters that are of interest to countries or continents and matters that are of interest only to the neighboring community, this underlying anxiety behind a rational climate of sociability, should not be confused with a stupid and unconscious surrender to the shapeless noise of a city. On the contrary, the site where he had decided to build his new house had not been chosen randomly. Situated a fair distance away from the closest neighborhood, the structure was surrounded, as has already been mentioned, by a concentration of nature that was not at all receptive to solitary walks, such was the impenetrable tangle of branches that sometimes seemed absolutely uncontrollable—almost as though they were demented. The possibility of larger objects passing through was even more remote. A mere shopping cart, for example, could use only a single possible trajectory to reach Walser's house. And that single path, which was, at any given moment, not broader than two meters, had to be defended—as though it were a damsel—not every day, of course, but definitely (at least) every month, from the silent but exceedingly effective advances of the forest.

From a certain moment onward, when the road led only to his house, once he had passed all the crossroads, Walser was keenly aware that he could count on nobody but himself to defend the small patch of organized earth that the fine materials of civilization had built. Even though legislation clearly stated that this was not his personal responsibility, but rather the responsibility of the community, Walser was sufficiently (albeit not deeply) acquainted with the ways of men to not nurture exaggerated illusions. He had therefore already bought a fairly large axe, which was safely ensconced (almost hidden) in one of the hardest rooms to access in his house. For Walser, this object was an almost inexcusable infiltration of aggressiveness in a space—his space—that had been built precisely to attract the opposite: cordiality, a handshake between two men who reach an understanding after a long argumentative chat, an emotional hug of farewell, and, possibly, who knows—Walser still nurtured this hope—a passionate kiss, an encounter with his definitive soul mate.

3

Walser was overjoyed! As soon as he opened the door to his house, he felt as though he was entering another world. As though it was not just a physical movement in space—a mere two steps—but was also a far more intense movement in time. From the rear foot that still bore the scent of the earth and the feeling, completely irrational but one that nonetheless exists, that one is surrounded by living things that we do not entirely understand and which do not understand us—elements of the forest—the distance between that rear foot and the foot that is in front, which has already stepped over the threshold of the door, should never be measured in centimeters, but in centuries, perhaps millennia. When he closed the door behind him, Walser felt he was turning his back on an inhuman bestiality (from which, it is true, billions of years ago, a creature endowed with an uncommon intelligence had emerged—that solitary builder known as Man) and was plunging head-on into the effects that this schism between humanity and the rest of nature had caused; a house in the middle of the forest, this was an absolutely rational conquest.

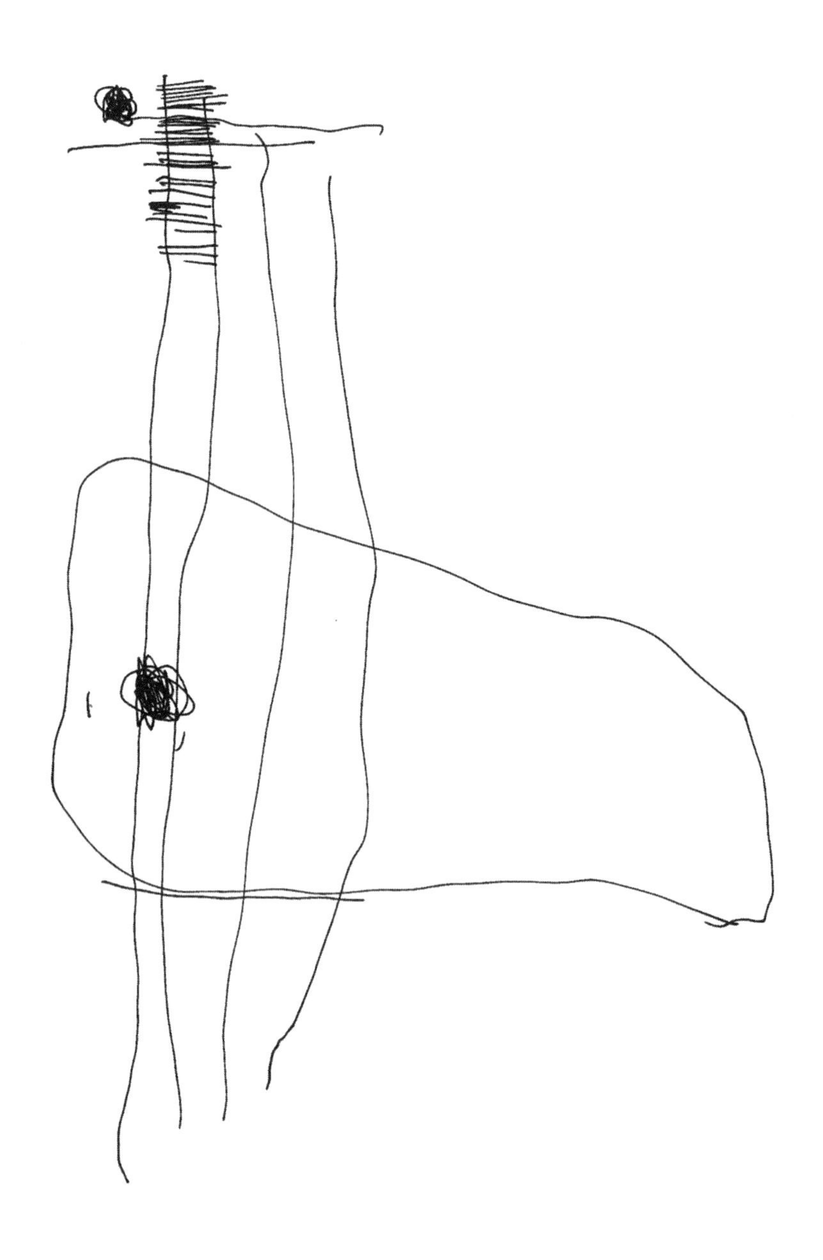

4

The smell of a new house was everywhere! A well-polished floor made of a light-colored wood ran through all the numerous rooms in the house, and there were said to be so many rooms that Walser had lost count; it was excessive, no doubt, but how can one criticize someone who was so enthused by his own expectations, someone who made the most of a plot of land that nobody wanted to build as large a structure as possible? Who knows what the future holds, thought Walser during the moments when he planned more rooms; who can guess what will happen during our lives? In fact, he had not built that house for the solitary man that he was at that point in time. Frankly speaking, without going into detail, Walser had great hopes for the future.

5

But such expectations had had consequences. Mister Walser sometimes became disoriented. He would go from one room to another and on to yet another and he sometimes found it difficult to find an object that he had left behind somewhere. But this merely amused him instead of irritating him! He felt like a child in such moments. It was at such moments that he realized that his entire adult existence had not conferred upon him any notion of judicious restraint; yes, he had exaggerated, but what else could he do: he was setting out on life, not ending it.

6

In the kitchen, out of curiosity, Walser ran his hand over the brick wall. One brick or another was jutting out more than the rest while others (of course) were set too far back, but on the whole they were more or less even. Near the floor, the small squares of the bricks finished serenely, without having needed to be amputated in the corners—all this was not just the work of a skilled hand, it was the result of mental skills, planning, knowing exactly how the job would finish at the moment it was started. Nothing had been improvised; undoubtedly, a fine job.

He then switched on the tap and without using a glass, bending his neck as he had done in his childhood, he drank the most delicious water that he could recall. He wiped away the drops that ran down his chin with his hand and almost let out a cry of sheer contentment for that moment, finally, of unambiguous solitude. There wasn't a single human sound to be heard.

And the baseboard that ran through the house, perfect! More than that: what aesthetic sense! What an uncanny understanding of the way in which color and shape should be combined, as though it (the baseboard) had existed that way in nature from the very outset.

Walser then sighed deeply, feeling that he had found something that he could never give up.

It is impossible to deem that movement that was almost a dance with which Walser caressed the furniture, turned doorknobs, and sat down on and got up from various chairs, as being excessive. He then sank into the gray sofa, a two-seater, already imagining his better half, the way he would brush away her hair from her face, how he would draw close to her. The stage was set. His new home!

Walser then sat down at the living-room table and wrote a letter that had seemed indispensable to him for many years, addressed to Thereza M. In the course of those handwritten lines he described the space, in a restrained manner, and invited her, with carefully chosen words, to visit him.

Each word in its place, each character written as though the very structure of the house, its foundations, depended on their shape. What concentration, that of Mister Walser!

Finally, even though his address was clearly written on the envelope, Walser did not hesitate to repeat it, and also drew a rudimentary map in the letter, with an enormous X marking the spot. He wanted to be absolutely sure that she—his Thereza—would be able to find her way to the door of his new home without getting lost.

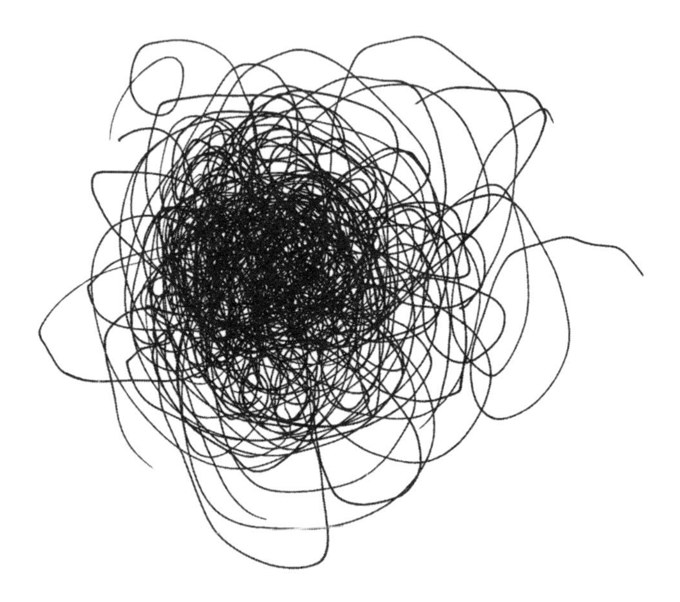

7

But, suddenly, somebody rang the doorbell. Who could it be? It couldn't be her—if Walser was still holding her letter in his hand. Only if . . .

Walser had been in his new home for not even two hours and his first visitor had already rung his doorbell, even before the first time he slept in his house—that first and somewhat uncomfortable sleep, thought Walser, given the circumstances, the casting aside of the pleasure that his body felt in this new space—he had a visitor. Before going to open the door he placed the letter in its envelope and closed it. Walser opened the door of his new home to let in a man who had arrived with all the air of someone who had not yet completed a certain task.

"What's the matter?" murmured Walser.

"It's the tap in the bathroom," said the man.

And he stepped into the house.

8

Perhaps he had been intoxicated with the novelty of the space, but he had certainly not noticed anything incomplete, either in the more or less concrete things that concerned his own being—that feeling of stability that involves muscles, respiratory rhythms, and an undeniable spirit of comfort that nobody could ever capture on paper—or things about the house. A tap had not yet been finished? Oh well, what did he know about such matters?

"Come in, my dear sir, take your time and conclude your work. . . . Nothing should be left half-finished," joked Walser to break the silence, but he got only an unintelligible murmur of agreement in response.

9

Having been removed from its fixture and placed on the floor, it almost seemed as though the tap was enjoying a moment of rest, and Walser felt a sudden urge to thank the man there and then, even before he finished his work. It felt like something that needed doing was being done, this was how calmly and definitively the tap and the ground had, in a manner of speaking, mixed.

Wielding a wrench, the man had first removed the nut that attached the tap to the pipe; then, after removing the tap, he had used a bit of liquid paraffin, perhaps, thought Walser, in order to improve the internal mechanisms; and everything then seemed to indicate that a new tap would emerge from his rectangular tool case, but it didn't.

"It's probably a leak," said the man.

Walser bent over the basin. He tried his best to feign as much interest as possible in the matter at hand, but in fact he was thinking of something else.

In truth, he was anxiously awaiting the moment in which he could once again sit in his new living room, savoring that unforgettable smell of paint and varnish that seems to have a well-defined dimension to it, not a material dimension, but a historical one—a smell that in a certain way seemed to be an analogy, in the physical world, of the expression that is a classic beginning to a narrative tale—the childish "Once upon a time." He wanted to start something and it was almost as though that man was getting in the way of it. He undoubtedly meant well, but a concrete obstacle had now appeared between Walser and his new life—the plumber.

Moreover, Walser hadn't a clue as to what was going on—the shape of those pipes did not stir him in the least. He saw them not as elements of a greater entity, which served a certain purpose, but simply as almost abstract forms. Since he did not understand the function of each element, Walser looked at the pipes as an aesthete would observe a hitherto unseen painting—trying to discern a meaning to it, not a utilitarian meaning but (so to speak) a spiritual one.

There was such a large gap between his thoughts and events around him that he saw the plumber's movements almost as though they were happening in a movie, as though there was a film between the two of them, and only one side, Walser's side, was real.

10

At that precise moment, Walser was interested in only one detail of what was happening beyond that screen: the number of objects and tools that the plumber had taken out of his case and had now left scattered all over the floor or on top of the basin. The greater the number of objects that were visible, the more time the man would take to leave. And, a few minutes ago, Walser had detected more things than were visible now. There was no doubt about it, the man's movements were like the ebbing of a tide, a withdrawal, which left Walser satisfied. He's about to leave, he thought.

In the meanwhile: the doorbell. Again.

Walser bowed slightly in a mute apology for absenting himself, and walked away from the plumber, who did not cease his activities for even a second.

Walser opened the door.

It was another man, with a toolkit in his hands.

"It's the floorboards."

Walser smiled, nodded his head, and let the man in.

11

No more than half an hour had passed when the doorbell rang for the third time.

It was a man who had come to fix something in the wall of one of the rooms. It seemed to be a crack.

He was immediately followed by another man. Walser hadn't even had the opportunity to shut the door. A window—it wasn't closing properly. Walser moved away from the door to allow the man to enter and followed him up to the window. Walser did not see anything wrong with the window in question, but it was clear that this new man, apart from being friendly and talkative, was a specialized technician.

"You were right to use bay windows, they're the easiest to open, but since the bolts run all along the window and slide into a groove, this sometimes creates an excessive gap right here, see? which can cause . . . I'm going to have to dismantle the window!" he exclaimed.

Perhaps he was about to object, who knows?, but the sound of the doorbell once again forced Walser to hurry away.

To have to dismantle a window (and that too on the first day), how unfortunate.

12

Over the course of the afternoon, all sorts of professionals continued to arrive. Between receiving them, which he tried to do as cordially as possible, and keeping track of the various repairs that were already under way, Walser, in a manner of speaking, forgot about himself.

As for the house, it gradually became unrecognizable, since the problems appeared to be worse than had been initially thought. Two windows had already been dismantled and had been temporarily substituted by cardboard, stuck to the walls with strong glue.

"It's not pretty, but it's only for a little while," somebody said, soothing Walser.

A little ahead, two or three men hunched over the floor were trying to adjust a series of floorboards that had been prized out, "due to seepage problems."

In fact, glancing through the length of the house, one could see that floorboards had been removed in several rooms.

In the meanwhile, a second man who specialized in plumbing was trying to unblock a sewage pipe, while the first plumber was patiently explaining to Walser that since it had been impossible to finish his work that day, it would be necessary to disconnect the water supply at least for a few days.

In their turn, the men who were working on the walls—repairing cracks and holes with cellulose filler—also said it would be impossible to finish that day. One of them described the difficulties involved in the task at length to Walser. If most of the small cracks could be covered up with filler and sandpapered, others required one or two extra coats of thick textured paint.

"Yes," agreed Walser. His new home still needed a few small repairs. So be it. What did he know about construction?!

"The electrical wiring has to be inspected thoroughly!" someone yelled from inside, apparently addressing Walser, but nobody would swear to the fact.

In fact, it had seemed, so they said, more like a shout making a general announcement; as though to alert a crowd and not just a single proprietor.

In the meanwhile, three men had already dismantled and were taking away parts of the gray sofa—the two-seater—in order to, as they duly informed him, "fix the springs."

At that moment, two men with grim, stony expressions crossed the room from one side to the other, muttering rather impolitely under their breath, protesting that the electrical wiring had been installed incorrectly from the very outset.

"You're not going to cut the power supply, are you?" asked Walser, smiling, but obviously afraid of the answer.

13

Nobody answered. Everybody was engaged in some gainful activity or the other. One of the men involved in the question of the electrical wiring around the house merely returned his smile; a smile that, from the corner of his lips, betrayed an obvious superiority in technical matters. Even a believer in the presence of an atheist could not have flashed a more satisfied grin.

In the meantime, several stepladders had already been scattered around the house, and some of the men were substituting roof panels that, they said, had mistakenly been glued to the slats.

"They should never have been glued," a man now explained to Walser. "The slats should either be fixed with nails or with brackets, never with glue; and they should be carefully spaced, with a gap of about 0.5 meters, at least, between them. Is this envelope yours, may I?"

Walser hesitated, he did not wish to seem rude, however, that letter was . . .

The man proceeded to go about his business, using the envelope to estimate the distance between the slats: "Well now, as you can see the gap here is far smaller."

"In addition . . . ," and he continued, however Walser, unfortunately, was unable to hear the rest of his explanation owing to an enormous crash that rang out from the other side of the house.

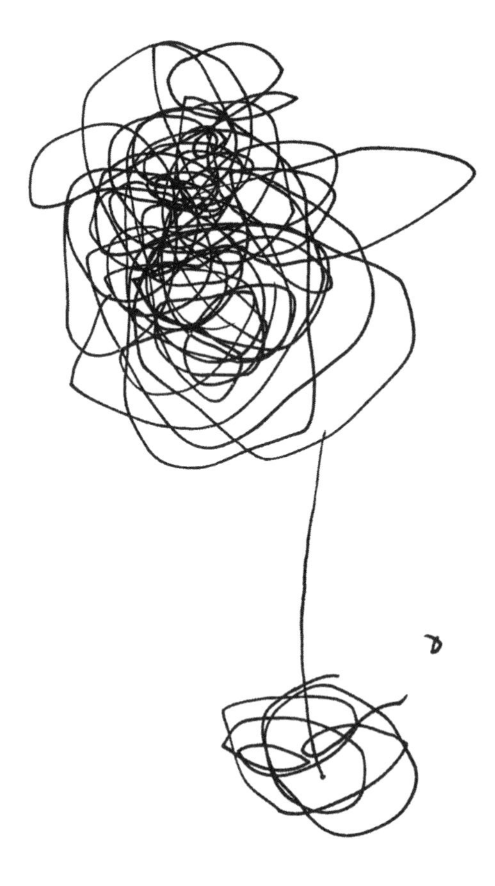

14

In fact, at first glance, it had seemed to him to be a little over the top (although it's true he was a layman) to destroy a wall simply because the electrical wiring had been badly installed from the outset, but what did he know about such matters?, he repeated to himself. However, he was unable to shake off a certain feeling of unease that engulfed him, for the first time, on that oh-so-important day on which he was inaugurating his new house. They could have at least informed me, thought Walser. Knocking down a wall, dammit, was something major.

"Was it really necessary?" asked Walser, standing a few meters away from a heap of broken bricks that were lying scattered all over and almost completely covered the floor in one of the rooms. "Was it because of the electrical wiring?"

"No, no," answered one of the men. "It's better this way, it facilitates movement. It provides a greater sense of comfort, we've joined these two rooms together and you now have a vast space."

"But why?!" gasped Walser, immediately disarmed by the man's smile and friendly insistence.

"It looks more beautiful this way."

In any case, it proved impossible to continue the conversation, since someone outside was urgently asking for Walser's presence. The latter, solicitous as ever, dutifully headed toward the grounds.

15

The pieces of wood that formed the scaffolding had been assembled there for a few hours now. Cut into more or less homogeneous pieces, with a width and length that enabled any man who climbed up there not to be alone, but allowed him only, at most, one partner, that too a well chosen one in terms of weight and width. Walser, accepting the way the world worked, without a murmur of objection, observed them being placed in the backyard of his new house.

Zealous workers, whom Walser could only admire, had prepared a structure in a matter of hours so that it was possible to climb up the back of the house, undoubtedly in order to repair some detail or other, although he did not know exactly what. Walser, now standing outside his house, could not help but feel moved by the immense concern with which these men sought to repair his newly inaugurated house.

He then observed the structure of the assembled scaffolding for a few moments—those alternating objects that masked a certain subtle wisdom inherent to that mixture of metal and wood.

Metal in the form of apparently barren pipes—without water, gas, or other material with a clear economic effectiveness—but nonetheless pipes that, essentially, enabled the most difficult of tasks: climbing to the top of his house without danger, or at least without an excessive degree of danger.

Of course, the scaffolding bothered him, aesthetically speaking.

It was just that his house was new. New not just in the sense that it had been built recently—what the devil, it hadn't even been a day—but also in the sense in which the youthfulness of an object is defined by a reasonable distance with regard to its demise. That house had a long career ahead of it, from that morning—the moment when it had been fully inaugurated. It was as though the scaffolding was heralding, or was itself, an external manifestation of a weakness, of something that wasn't working, of the need for repairs.

His profession, however, was something quite different—certainly each one of those steps had a technical significance that he would never have dared to dispute—he had always respected the destiny and inclinations of each individual's profession.

Finally, one of the men came over.

"What's that for?" asked Walser, pointing to the scaffolding.

"It's the roof," answered the man.

"It has a hole in it."

16

It was an apparently harmless crack in the attic.

Walser came back to the house and went upstairs to confirm this. It was his new house, dammit. And now there was a crack in the roof! "A small crack, infinitesimal," they had said. Yes, but it was a crack. He was going to see it with his own eyes.

Upon reaching the attic he climbed up on a bench that two men, in consideration of his evident ineptness in such matters, amiably secured for him—one holding each side.

"See for yourself!" they had said to Walser, seemingly sorrowful about the fact.

Standing on the bench, Walser stretched his legs as far as he could, then his arms, and finally his fingers. A hole! In his new roof. It was a fact.

But of course the crack was not just that: something that wasn't there. On the contrary, very much to the contrary: at that moment Walser felt that some element was coming out of there—some material that hit him on the head from on top. Like a mischievous child, it hit him once, then again, and hid in a trice.

Where? How was he to find out? Perhaps on top of the roof, at that blind angle that Walser would never be able to glimpse from there?

In the meanwhile, the hammering increased, so to speak, in intensity. What had first appeared merely to be the effect of an errant breeze, adrift from the sensible course of its community, was now, to Walser, an evident threat.

But what did he really feel—he who, until then, had been so serene, enjoying his first day in his new house? Just this: a fragile premonition popped into his head and an equally fragile proposal—or rather a temptation—coming from outside, making the most of precisely that unexpected crack in the roof of the attic, infiltrating into the house, touching him, pulling him, beckoning him to an action that Walser had not yet quite managed to define, but which he felt was located in that vast and, once finally inside, unending, field of evil.

He got down from the bench; and one of the men flashed a strange grin.

"Yes," agreed Walser, "this has to be closed."

17

The first man to request permission to sleep there in Walser's house that night was one of the electricians. Subsequently, many other workmen repeated the request.

It had already grown dark and the agglomeration of houses down there, the closest neighborhood to the house, was still many kilometers away and was far from being the safest route to travel at night. Although Walser was already tired, he concentrated all his energy on being hospitable: he fetched blankets, found two mattresses, cushions—in short, he did his best to ensure that nobody felt uncomfortable in his house. At a certain point he even felt that the best thing to do was to leave the men to sort things out for themselves—each one finding his own corner to rest comfortably. Apart from which, they no longer asked his permission for anything. He tried not to pay too much heed to this fact. This was also because—owing to the tools, the bricks and various other objects scattered all over the floor, and the vast clouds of dust that made it difficult to see—it was hard to move around, and many of the men who were in the farthest rooms would have found it difficult to make their way to the room where he was.

The space no longer allowed much room for manners.

"Let them all sleep there," thought Walser, without suppressing his characteristic sense of protectiveness. "It's already dark outside!"

With a lit candle in his hand—since the electricity really had been disconnected—and carefully skirting the various human and material obstacles scattered all over the place (a snore or two could already be heard), Walser tried to find his way to his room and thus finally reach his bed. So that he could then sleep for the first time in his house, always a significant event.

After various attempts to find his room, Walser gave up. Both on account of the darkness, which his candle and some other candles scattered throughout the house were unable to dispel, as well as due to some concrete, physical changes—dismembered walls, new walls that had begun to be built in places that had earlier allowed passage.

At that point he was just too exhausted. He decided to lie down right there, in what appeared to be a corridor, although it was not very narrow. Not having foreseen this turn of events he had neglected to bring his coat from the hall. It was quite cold there owing to the fact that some windows had been removed from their frames and the cardboard covering these gaps was insufficient.

Attempting to overcome a certain embarrassment, Walser approached a man who was snoring a few meters away from him and with slow and careful movements pulled toward him the small blanket that (and this thought soothed his conscience) had slipped off the man's feet, thus ceasing to serve its purpose.

Completely wrapped in the blanket and propped against one of the walls—from which, he noted, they had removed the baseboard—after such a long day, despite being parched with thirst, Walser finally fell asleep, serenely, thinking about the next day. He had great hopes for the future.

About the Author and Illustrator

Of novelist **Gonçalo M. Tavares,** professor of epistemology at the University of Lisbon, Nobel laureate José Saramago declared, "Tavares has no right to be writing so well at the age of thirty-five. One feels like punching him." Tavares is the winner of numerous international awards, including the Brazilian Prêmio Portugal Telecom in 2007 for *Jerusalém* and the 2010 Prix du Meilleur Livre Étranger for *Apprendre à prier à l'ère de la technique* (*Aprender a Rezar na Era da Técnica / Learning to Pray in the Age of Technique*).

Rachel Caiano is a Portuguese artist and illustrator of fiction, children's literature, book covers, and other publications.